Hugh Conway

Bound Together

Vol. 1

Hugh Conway

Bound Together
Vol. 1

ISBN/EAN: 9783337343163

Printed in Europe, USA, Canada, Australia, Japan

Cover: Foto ©Andreas Hilbeck / pixelio.de

More available books at **www.hansebooks.com**

BOUND TOGETHER.

TALES.

BY

HUGH CONWAY,

(F. J. FARGUS,)

AUTHOR OF 'CALLED BACK.'

IN TWO VOLUMES.

VOL. I.

London:

REMINGTON AND CO.,

HENRIETTA STREET, COVENT GARDEN.

1884.

TO MY FRIEND,

JOSEPH L. ROECKEL.

CONTENTS.

* These three tales were originally published in *Blackwood's Magazine.*

BOUND TOGETHER.

THE

SECRET OF THE STRADIVARIUS.

My friend Luigi is reckoned one of the finest violin-players of the day. His wonderful skill has made him famous, and he is well known and honoured for his talent in every capital in Europe.

If in these pages I call him by a name other than the one he has made famous, it is solely on account of a promise he exacted from me, in case I should ever feel tempted to make the following strange experiences, we shared together, public property. I am afraid, nevertheless, that too many will readily identify the man himself with the portrait I am obliged to draw.

VOL. I.   1

Luigi—leaving his professional greatness
out of the question—would have been a
noticeable man in any company, a man at
whom people would look and ask not only,
' Who is he ?' but ' What has he done in the
world ?' knowing that men of his stamp are
seldom sent upon this scene to live an
ordinary everyday life.   In person he was
very tall, standing over six feet.   His figure
graceful : some might even have called it
slight, there was breadth of shoulder enough
to tell it was the figure of a strong man.   A
face with a pale but clear complexion ; dark
deep-set eyes, with a sort of far-away expression in them ; black hair, worn long, after the
manner of geniuses of his kind ; a high but
rugged forehead ; a well-shaped nose ; a
drooping moustache ; a hand whose long
and delicate fingers seemed constructed expressly for their particular mission—violin-
playing.

Picture all these characteristics, and if you
enjoy the acquaintance of the musical world,
or even if you have been in the habit of
attending concerts where stars of the first
magnitude condescend to shine, I fear, in

spite of my promise of concealing his name, you will too easily recognise my friend.

Luigi's manner in ordinary life was very quiet, gentlemanly, and reposed. He was, in his dreamy sort of way, highly courteous and polite to strangers. Although, when alone with me or other friends he loved, he had plenty to say for himself—and his broken English was pleasant to listen to—in general company he spoke but little. But let his left hand close round the neck of a fiddle, let his right hand grasp the bow, and one knew directly for what purpose Luigi came into the world. Then the man lived and re-velled, as it were, in a life of his own making. The notes his craft drew forth were like bracing air to him; he seemed actually to respire the music, and his dreamy eyes awoke and shone with fire. He did that rare thing—rare indeed, but lacking which no performer can rise to enduring fame—threw his whole soul into his playing. His manner, his very attitude as he com-menced, was a complete study.

Drawing himself up to every inch of his height, he placed the violin—nestling it, I may say—under his chin, and then taking a long breath of what appeared to be anticipatory pleasure, swept his magician's wand over the sleeping strings, and waking them with the charmed touch, wove his wonderful spell of music. The moment the horsehair came in contact with the gut, the listener knew that he was in the presence of a master.

Luigi had come to London for the season, having, after much negotiation and persuasion, accepted an engagement at a long series of some of the best, if cheapest and most popular concerts held in London. It was his first visit to England:he had ever disliked the country, and believed very little in the national love for good music, or in our power of appreciating it when heard. He disliked, also, the trumpeting with which the promoters of the concerts heralded his appearance. Although his fame was already great throughout the Continent, he dreaded the effect of playing to an unsympathetic audience. His fears were, however, groundless.

Whether the people liked and understood his music and style of playing or not, they least appeared to do so ; and the newspapers, one and all, unable to do things by halves, went into raptures over him. They compared him with Paganini, Ole Bull, and other bygone masters, and their comparisons were very flattering. Altogether, Luigi was a great success.

I met him on two occasions at the houses of some friends of mine, who are in the habit of spending much time, trouble, and some money on that strange sport, lion-hunting. His concerts were held, I think, on two evenings in every week ; so he had time at his disposal, and was somewhat sought after. We were introduced, and I took a liking to the quiet, gentlemanly celebrity, who, different from many others whose names are in the mouths of men, gave himself no airs, nor vaunted, by words or manner, the 'aristocracy of talent.'

I could make shift to converse with him fairly enough in his own soft language ; so that upon my meeting him the second time, he expressed his pleasure at again encountering me. A few days afterwards we met by chance in the street, and I was able to extricate him from some little difficulty, into which his imperfect knowledge of English and of English ways had betrayed him. Then our acquaintance ripened, until it became friendship; and even at this day I reckon him amongst the friends I hold the dearest.

I saw a great deal of Luigi during his stay in London. We made pleasant little excursions together to such objects of interest as he wished to visit. We spent many evenings together, nights I should rather say, for the small hours had sounded when we parted, leaving the room dim with the smoke from my cigars and his cigarettes. Like many of his countrymen, he smoked simply whenever he could get a chance; and when alone with me, I believe the only cessation to his consumption of tobacco was when he took his beloved fiddle in his hand and played for his own pleasure and my delight.

He was a charming companion—indeed what man who had seen such varied life as he had, could be otherwise when drawn out by the confidence that friendship gives? I soon found that under the external calmness

of the man lay a nature full of poetry, and
not free from excitement. I was also much
amused to find a vivid vein of superstition
and belief in the supernatural running
through his character; and I believe it was
only my merriment on making the discovery that hindered him from expatiating
upon some ghostly experiences he had himself gone through, instead of darkly hinting
at what he could reveal. It was in vain I
apologised for my ill-timed mirth, and with a
grave face tried to tempt him. He only
said: 'You, like the rest of your cold-
blooded, money-making race, are sceptical,
my friend. I will tell you nothing. You
would not believe : you would laugh at me—
and ridicule is death to me.'

Another thing about which he was very
tenacious was showing his skill when invited
out. He invariably declined to do so, seeming quite puzzled by the polite hints thrown
out by some of his entertainers.

'Why can they not come and hear me
in public ?' he asked me. 'Or can it be that
they only ask me to their houses for my
talents, not for my society ?'

I told him I was afraid their motives were rather mixed ; so he said quietly :

'Then I shall not go out again. When I do not play in public to earn my living, I play for myself alone.'

He kept his resolve as well as he could— declining all of his many invitations, save those to a few houses where he knew he was valued, as he wished to be, for himself.

But when I was alone with him, when I visited him at his rooms, then he was not chary in showing his skill ; and, although I blush to say so, at times I had violin-playing *ad nauseam*. A surfeit of sweets—a satiety of music. I often wonder if it has ever been any man's lot to hear such performances as I did in those days when, grown careless of the good the gods would send me, I lay at full length on Luigi's sofa ; and the master of the magic bow expounded themes in a manner which would have brought the house down. Till then I little dreamt of what, in skilful hands, the instrument could do. How true genius could bid it laugh, sob, command, entreat—sink into a wail of pathetic pleading, or soar to a song of scorn and triumph ! what

power to express every emotion of the heart
lay in those few inches of cunningly curved
wood ! Now I could understand why Luigi
could play so much for his own enjoyment ;
and at times it seemed to me that his execution was even more wonderful, his expression
more thrilling, when I alone formed his
audience, than when a vast assembly was
before him, ready, as the last impassioned
notes sank into silence, to break into a storm
of rapturous applause.

Luigi was a connoisseur in fiddles, and
owned several pet instruments by the most
renowned makers. Sometimes of an evening
he would bring out his whole stock, look
them carefully over, play a little on each, and
point out to me the difference in the tone.
Then he would wax eloquent on the peculiar
charms or gifts the master's hand had be-
stowed on each, and was indignant that I
was so obtuse as not to detect at once the
exquisite gradations of the graceful curves.
After a short time the names of Amati,
Ruggieri, Guarnerius, Klotz, Stainer, etc.,
grew quite familiar to me ; and as I went
through the streets I would peep into the

pawnbrokers' and other windows with fiddles
in them, hoping to pick up a treasure for a
few shillings.   Two or three I did buy, but
my friend laughed so heartily at my pur-
chases that I gave up the pursuit.

He told me he had for a long while been
looking for a genuine old Stradivarius, but,
as yet, had not succeeded in finding the one
he wanted.   He had been offered many,
purporting to have come originally from the
great maker's hands, but probably they were
all pretenders, as he was not yet suited.

One evening when I visited Luigi I found
him with all his musical treasures arrayed
around him.   He was putting them in order,
he said. I must amuse myself as best I could
until he had finished.   I turned idly from
one case to another, wondering how any
experience could determine the build of any
particular violin, all of which, to my un-
tutored eyes, appeared alike.   Presently I
opened one case which was closed, and drew
the fiddle it held from its snug, red-lined bed.
I did not remember having seen this one
before, so took it in my hand to examine it—
holding it, after the manner of connoisseurs,

edgeways before my eyes to note the curves and shape of it. It was evidently old—my little knowledge told me that; and as, even though protected by the case, dust lay upon it, I could see it had not been used for a long, long time. Moreover, all the strings were broken. Curiously, each one was severed at exactly the same point—just below the bridge —as if some one had passed a sharp knife across, and with one movement cut all four.

Holding the ill-used instrument towards Luigi, I said :

' This one seems particularly to want your attention. Is it a valuable one ?'

Luigi, who was engrossed by the delicate operation of shifting the sounding-post of one of his pet weapons some infinitesimal part of an inch to the left or to the right, turned as I spoke, still holding his ends of string in each hand. As soon as he saw which violin I had taken up, he let fall the one he held between his knees, and, to my great surprise, said hastily :

' Put it down—put it down, my friend. I beseech you not to handle that violin.'

Rather annoyed at the testy way in which

my usually amiable friend spoke, I laid it down, saying :

'Is it so precious, then, that you are afraid of my clumsy hands damaging it ?'

'Ah, it is not that,' answered Luigi ; 'it is something altogether different.   I did not know my man had brought that fiddle in.   I never intended it should have left Italy.'

'It looks an old one.   Who is it by ?'

'That is a real old Stradivarius—the acme of mortal skill--the one thing human hands have made in this world perfect—perfect as a flower, perfect as the sea.   A Stradivarius is the only thing that cannot be altered—cannot be improved upon.'

'Why do you never use it ?'

'I cannot tell you—you would not believe me.   There is a something about that fiddle I cannot explain.   I believe it to be the finest in the world.   It may be even that Manfredi played upon it to Boccherini's 'cello.   It may be Kruger led with it when the mighty applause rang through the Kärntnerthor, shaking it from floor to roof-tree, but which he, the grand deaf genius, Beethoven, could not even hear.   Who can tell what hands have used it ? and yet, alas ! I dare not play upon it again.'

Rendered very curious by Luigi's enigmatical words and excited manner, I ventured to take the violin in my hands again, and examined it with interest.   I looked carefully at the belly and the back, noting the beautiful red but translucent varnish, known alone to Stradivarius, with which the latter was coated.   I peeped through the ff's, to ascertain if any maker's name appeared inside.   If one had ever been there, it was completely obliterated by a dark stain, which covered the greater portion of the inside of the back. Luigi offered no remonstrance as I took the fiddle for the second time, but sat silent, watching me with apparent interest.

And now a strange thing occurred to me— let who can explain it.   After holding that fiddle for a few minutes, I felt a wish—an impulse—growing stronger and stronger each moment, till it became almost irresistible—to play upon it.   It was not a musician's natural itching to try a fine old violin—indeed, I am no musician, although fond of listening to music, and at times venturing to criticise ;

neither have I learnt nor attempted to learn
the art of performing on any instrument,
from the Jew's-harp to the organ. And yet,
I say, as my fingers were round the neck—as
soft as silk it was—of that old violin, not only
did I feel a positive yearning to pass the bow
across it, but somehow I was filled with the
conviction, odd as it was, that all at once I
was possessed of the power of bringing rare
music forth. So strong, so intense was this
feeling, that, heedless of the ridicule from my
companion to which I should expose myself
—heedless, indeed, of his presence—I cuddled
the fiddle under my chin, and took up one of
the several bows lying on the table. My
left fingers fell instinctively into their proper
position on the strings, or rather, where the
strings should have been ; and then I remembered the ruined state those strings were in,
and, with all my new-born skill, knew that no
miraculous inspiration, even if it produced a
fiddler, could bring forth music from wood
alone. Yet the impulse was on me stronger
than ever ; and, absurd as it may seem, I
turned to Luigi with the request on my lips
that he would restring the useless instrument.

Luigi had been watching me attentively ; no doubt he had studied every motion, every vagary of mine since I again began to handle the fiddle.   Seeing me turn towards him, he sprang from his seat, and before I could speak, snatched the fiddle from my hands, replacing it at once in its case ; then closing the cover, he heaved a deep sigh of relief.   I had no time to entreat, remonstrate, or resist ; but as he took the fiddle from me, all wish to distinguish myself in a line that was not my own left me, and I almost laughed aloud at the folly and presumption of which I had been mentally guilty.   Yet it was strange—very strange.

'Ah !' said Luigi, as he placed the fiddle out of sight under the table, 'so you felt it also, my friend ?'

'Felt what ?'

'The—I don't know what to call it—the power, the sorcery of it.'

'I felt—don't laugh at me—that had the strings been there, I, who never played a fiddle in my life, could have drawn exquisite music from that one.   What does it mean ?'

Luigi returned no answer to my inquiry, but said, as if thinking aloud :

'So it was no dream of mine. He, the cool, collected Englishman—he felt it also. He could not resist the impulse. It was no dream—no creation of my fancy. Would he see it, I wonder ?'

'See what ?' I asked, curious to know what his wandering sentences meant.

'I cannot tell you. You would not believe me.'

'But what do you mean by the sorcery of the fiddle ?'

'Did I say sorcery ?—Well, I know no other word that can describe it. Although I tell you I believe that fiddle is the finest in the world, I have only played upon it twice ; and the second time I drew my knife across the strings, that I might never again be tempted to play upon it without due consideration.'

'What is its history, then ? Where did you get it ?' I asked, by this time thinking my friend was suffering from some eccentricity that genius occasionally exhibits.

'It was sent me originally from London. When I found out its secret, I begged my agent in England to ascertain its history.

After some trouble, he traced it to a house where, for many years, it had lain unnoticed in a garret. That house had once been a lodging-house ; so doubtless the fiddle had belonged to some one who had sojourned there for a time. I could learn no more about it, save what it told me in its music.'

I saw Luigi was far away from any wish to jest, so paused before I asked him the meaning of his last sentence. He anticipated me, and said :

' You wonder at my words. Did you notice nothing else strange about it ?'

' Only a dark stain inside ; as if wine had been spilt into it.'

' Ah !' cried Luigi excitedly, ' that is it ! that is the secret—the meaning of the power it holds. If it were not for the varnish that fiddle would be stained outside and inside. That stain is from a man's heart's blood, and that fiddle can tell how and why he died.'

' I do not understand you.'

' I do not expect you to—or believe me— why should you ? What have you, an un- imaginative Anglo-Saxon, to do with marvels? How, in the centre of a great, cruel, material

city, with the ceaseless sound of traffic outside our windows, should you expect anything
supernatural? It may be I only dreamt it.
Perhaps you would not see it. And yet, one
night when I feel strong enough, we will take
the fiddle from its case, and I will play it to
you—I who, until to-night, have not laid a
finger on it for five years. And then, if its
music moves you as it moved me, I dreamt
no dream. If not, I will say it was a dream,
and I may at last be able to use this masterpiece of Stradivarius.'

I begged him to name an early day for the
curious performance, but he would make no
promise; so we parted for the night.

A month passed by: Luigi's London engagement terminated, and he was now going
to win fresh laurels at Berlin. I had seen
him two or three times every week, but he
had never referred to the conversation which
had taken place upon the night when I drew
the strange violin from its case; nor had he
offered to redeem his promise made on that
occasion. I had ceased to think about it, or
indeed only remembered it as a jest, laughing
at the idea of a superstitious man not being

able to play on any particular fiddle. Two days before he left England he wrote me asking me to dine with him that night, adding, 'I think I may keep my promise of playing upon the Stradivarius.'

We dined at a well-known restaurant, and about ten o'clock went to Luigi's rooms to finish the night. The first thing I saw, upon entering, was the fiddle-case lying on the table—Luigi's favourite bow and several coils of strings beside it. We sat down and talked on various topics for about an hour, and then I said :

'I see you have made preparations for the performance. When do you intend to begin ?'

Luigi drew a deep breath. 'My friend,' he said, 'you will not blame me if my playing agitates you; and remember, when I once begin I must continue to the end. It is no pleasure to me—it is rather deadly pain. But I am curious, and would satisfy my doubts.'

He was so much in earnest that I checked the laugh his solemn manner called up, and merely nodded acquiescence. He then rose, and saying, 'We must not be interrupted,' called his servant, and after giving him the necessary

instructions, locked the door, placing the key
in his pocket. He then opened the mysterious case, and with tender hands drew forth
the violin. His nimble fingers soon detached
the severed strings, knotted on the new ones,
and in the course of about a quarter of an
hour the instrument was ready, and tuned to
his satisfaction. I felt, as I watched him, I
should like to take the violin in my hands
once more, to see if the strange desire I had
before experienced would again come over
me—but I hardly liked to ask him to permit
me to do so.

And now all was ready—Luigi's critical ear
satisfied with the sound of the strings—and
he seemed about to strike his favourite attitude. Yet I noticed his pale face was paler
than usual, and the hand poising the bow
seemed tremulous ; and as I looked at him, a
sympathetic feeling of fear—a dread of something, I knew not what—crept over me. It
seemed too absurd, however, to be disturbed
by an excitable Italian playing a violin in a
room with all the appliances of modern everyday life around me ; so I laughed away the
feeling, placed myself at full length on the

sofa—my favourite attitude for listening to the
master's performances—and was prepared to
give my undivided attention to the music.

And yet, for a while Luigi did not begin,
although he saw I had resigned myself to
my fate. He had placed the violin under
his chin ; his left-hand fingers were on the
strings, but for some minutes he contented
himself with beating a sort of time, or
rhythmical measure, with the bow. One
would have said he was endeavouring to
recall something he had heard once, and
only imperfectly remembered.

'What theme are you going to play to
me ?' I asked.

On hearing my voice he looked at me
vacantly, and only upon my repeating the
question did he seem aware of my presence.
Then with an effort he said, ceasing not to
beat time the while :

'Ah, that I do not know. I am no longer
my own master ; I cannot choose. Let me
beg of you not to interrupt me again, my
friend.'

I said no more, but watched him with
anxious eyes. The left-hand fingers slipped,

slid, and danced in dumb show up and down the strings, the bow for ever beating time. A sort of shiver passed over him; then, drawing himself up, he swept the bow across the strings, and the fiddle, silent for so many years, found tongue at last.

A weird strain, commanding the listener's attention at once—a strain I knew I had never heard before. So curious the opening bars sounded, that, had I dared, I should have said that several well-established rules of harmony were outraged. And yet, in spite of its peculiarity, I knew that he who created that music was a master in the art. It was not Wagner, I was sure, although somewhat of his remarkable power of expression, and gift of moving the mind without the aid of melody, was present. The first thirty bars, or so, appeared to me to be of the nature of an overture, heralding the performance to follow. In snatches of mystic music the violin spoke of joy and sorrow, pain and pleasure, love and hate, hope and fear; and as my own thoughts responded to the varied emotions, I lay and wondered who could have written the music

which affected me so; and thought how
fortunate the unknown composer was to have
such an exponent of his ideas as Luigi.
Yet, as I looked at the latter, it struck me
his style of playing to-night was different
from usual. Faultless though the execution
was—marvellous as were the strains those
facile fingers drew forth—the whole manner
of the man seemed to be mechanical, utterly
at variance with the fire and dash that ever
characterized his performances. The skill
was there, but, for once, the soul was wanting. With the exception of his hands and
arms, he stood so still that he might have
been a statue. He played as one in a trance,
and his eyes with a fixed look were ever
directed towards the end of the apartment.
Swifter and swifter his arm flew backwards
and forwards—more strange, eccentric, and
weird the music became—stronger in its
expression, plainer in its eloquence, more
thrilling in its intensity, and ever exercising
its powerful spell on the hearer. At last,
with a sort of impulse, I turned my eyes
from the player and looked in the direction
in which he looked. Suddenly the music

changed.　There was now no lack of melody.
A soft, soothing, haunting measure began—
a sort of dreamy far-away tune; and as its
gentle cadences fell on my ear, hitherto kept
in a state of irritating, if not unpleasing,
expectation, my thoughts began to wander to
old and half-forgotten scenes—distant events
came to my mind—recollections of vanished
faces, once familiar, flocked around me—all
things seemed growing misty and indistinct,
and I felt as one sinking into sleep—the sort
of sleep that one can almost realize and
enjoy.

It was not to be, however.　A few harsh
notes from the fiddle, sounding like a warning or admonition, recalled me to wakeful-
ness; and as my straying thoughts collected
themselves, that lulling song began again.

And yet, if fully awake and conscious,
where was I?　The scene was entirely
changed; and although I knew I was still
lying where I had at first placed myself—
although I could hear within a few feet of
me the unceasing melody of Luigi's violin
—I was now looking into a strange apartment, even as one looks into the representa-

tion of a room on the stage; and I knew I
was dreaming no dream. It could be none;
for, as I gazed, I felt a feeling of utter
astonishment—and that feeling is always
absent from a dream, however marvellous
its features may be. Yet, lying there, and
in as full possession of my faculties as I am
at the moment of writing these words, I saw,
opened as it were before me, a strange room,
and one I could in no way connect with any
chamber which I was in the habit of entering.
It appeared to be a large, lofty apartment;
and if I was looking at a vision, neither the
room nor its belongings presented any appearance of unreality. The latter, indeed,
gave the idea of wealth and comfort. The
furniture was after the fashion of the early
part of this century. The chairs were
covered with costly old brocade; and a
short, square pianoforte—then the highest
triumph of the maker's art—stood open
against one wall. And as, with the sound of
the violin ever near me, I noted these things
and waited for what was to come, I knew—
although I did not attempt it—that I was
utterly powerless to turn my eyes from the

phantom scene before me, even to ascertain
whether it could be that Luigi saw the
things I saw.

Another change in the wonder-working
music. A long rippling *legato* passage,
sweeping into a tender, passionate, pleading
strain—the eloquent notes speaking of joy
and fear mingled. As my heart followed and
understood the inspiration of the musician,
I whispered to myself, ' This is love.' As if
in answer to my thoughts, the door of the
phantom room opened, and two figures entered
—a lady and a gentleman. Both wore the
dresses of that period to which I have
assigned the date of the furniture, and both
were young. Like the objects around them,
there was nothing in their appearance ghost-
like or supernatural. Their limbs looked as
firm and round as my own. It was some
little time before I could take my eyes from
the girl. She was supremely beautiful—tall
and fair, with a delicate, refined face ; and
the robe she wore plainly showed the exquisite proportions of her figure. Her companion was handsome, but his features wore
an expression of melancholy pride. I noticed

he carried under his left arm a violin, and
something told me he was a Frenchman.
With great courtesy he led the girl to a seat,
and, as if in obedience to a request of hers,
commenced playing the instrument. Still
the same sweet strain fell on my ears; but
a stranger thing than any I had yet noticed
was that, as he played, the sound seemed to
come from his violin, and Luigi's was dumb.
And as he played, the girl looked up at him
with admiring eyes. He ceased at last, and
Luigi's fiddle immediately resumed the
melody, without a moment's break. Then
I saw the phantom place the violin and bow
in the girl's hands, instructing her how to
hold them; and I knew that, during the
lesson, his voice as well as his eyes made
avowal of his passionate love. I saw his
fingers linger on hers as he placed them on
the strings; I saw the blush deepen upon
her cheek, the lashes droop over her down-
cast eyes, and then I saw him lean over and
press his lips to the fair white hand which
held the bow; whilst the music near me,
sinking almost to silence, and tremulous as
if a man's future lay on those vibrating

strings, told me he sought his fate at her
lips. He threw himself at her feet, and I
saw the girl bend over him, and placing her
arms around his neck, kiss his forehead,
whilst high and loud rose the song of sweet
triumph from those impassioned chords,
doubtful of her love no longer.

Again the strain changed—a song of love
no longer: a few notes of warning, melting
into a strain that foretold and spoke of
sorrow. Again I saw the door of the
apartment open, and, with a hasty step,
another man entered. He, too, was young
and powerfully built, with an intensely
English face. Yet I could trace in his
harder features a resemblance, such as a
brother might bear, to the girl before me.

As he entered, the lovers sprang to their
feet; then, covering her face with her hands,
the girl sank upon a chair, whilst her companion faced the new-comer with an air as
haughty as his own, and words of scorning,
of contempt, of shaming, of defiance, were
hurled from man to man. True, I heard
them not—all the phantasmagoria came before me in dumb show; but the varied tones

of the violin told me all that passed between the two men as truly as though their voices smote upon my ear ; and, as the wild music culminated in a fierce *crescendo* of thrilling power, the two men grappled in their rage, and the girl sprang to her feet and ran wildly to the door.

For a moment all grew misty, and the phantom actors of my vision were hidden from my sight. When they reappeared, I saw the young Frenchman quitting the room, with blood trickling down his pale cheek ; and as, with a look of undying hate on his face, he closed the door behind him, the room and all faded from my sight.

But no pause in the music ; still those weird notes weaving the mystic spell that chained me. Leaving me no time to reflect on what I had seen, but enforcing my attention to the drama acted before me, the fiery *crescendo* sank in a dull sullen theme, almost colourless when compared with the foregoing numbers ; then, as with dissolving views, where one scene grows through another that fades, I began to realize that I looked into another room—one very different from the first.

It was evidently, from the slanting roof and small window, an attic, and its contents spoke of poverty. A bedstead with thread-bare hangings occupied one corner, and in the centre, at a square table littered with sheets of music, sat the young Frenchman. His brow was contracted, and the wound yet fresh on his cheek. He was writing, and through the medium of the music I knew the purport of his epistle as well as if I had looked over his shoulder. It was a chal-lenge—a challenge, which, he stated, his late antagonist dare not decline, as the writer was of even more noble family than the man who had insulted him.

Having written the letter, he rose and paced the small room, deep in thought. As his steps went backwards and forwards across the limited space—as his thoughts grew black with hate as he remembered the insult he had suffered, or grew bright with love as he pictured the fair girl who had pledged herself to him—so truthfully did the delicate gradations of the music harmonize with them, that I could feel every emotion stirring his heart, at times almost identifying myself

with him—making his joy, his sorrow,
mine.

After what seemed to be hours, he took up
the violin that lay on the table near him, and
commenced playing.   As before, I say,
whether Luigi's hands produced it or not,
the sound came from him ; and as he played,
the music, at first fierce, stern, and harsh,
gradually toned down until it became dreamy
and lulling—until at last he threw himself on
his poor bed, and Luigi's violin resumed the
strain—the soft, soothing measure I have
before mentioned, telling of placid sleep.

Another change—hard, sharp, *staccato* pas-
sages. I was now looking—it might be from
a window—on a wide expanse of smooth
green turf. As before, the scene was so real,
so material, that I might have stepped out
on to the sward. There was nothing in the
locality which I could identify. A wall and
some palings, I remember, were on the left
hand ; a belt of trees on the right. As I
looked, I saw figures at some little distance.

Two men in their shirt-sleeves were engaged in a deadly duel. They were not so
far away but I could plainly distinguish their

features ; and I knew they were those of the
two men whom I had seen grapple in the room.
As their slender, flashing blades twined in
and out like serpents—as they thrust and par-
ried, advanced and retreated—the mysterious
music entered fully into the fray, accompanying every stroke, until, as the arm of one of
the combatants sank by his side, helpless—
pierced by his antagonist's blade—it swelled
to a strain of exultation.

It was the Englishman who was wounded;
and as the sword dropped from his grasp, his
opponent with difficulty checked the impulse
urging him to drive his weapon through his
unguarded breast; then, seeing his foe was
quite unable to renew the combat, bowed with
cold politeness, sheathed his sword, and turned
away, leaving the wounded man to the care
of his second. As the Frenchman vanished
from my sight among the trees at the right
hand, the scene grew blurred and faded—only
the spell of the music continued ever.

The dismal measure and the dismal garret
once more. As I look at the poverty-
stricken room, the music, eloquent as before,
in some hidden manner makes me aware that

months have passed since I last looked at it. The young Frenchman is present. Indeed, I begin now to understand that no scene can come beneath my eyes unless he be an actor in it. It is his life, his love, the violin in its own marvellous tongue relates. I wait with interest now. I have no time to wonder at or speculate upon what I have seen ; no time to endeavour to explain the phantom scenes and actions which the song of the Stradi-varius has brought before me. I feel no fear —curiosity and excitement only. Luigi's presence I have forgotten, so intent am I upon the drama played before me.

The young man, I notice, is handsome as ever, but paler, thinner, and careworn. What is the music saying now in that strange speech which I interpret so readily ? Poverty and hopelessness, loss of love, and with that loss the wish to rise to fame.

He is writing ; but the paper before him this time is a score—the score of a work he once thought would hand his name down to future times. Well I know, as I watch him, that music will never be given to the world. I know it is night ; and to kill his bitter

thoughts he is sitting down and working
without interest at his uncompleted score.
As I watch him, grieving at his grief, weird
and dreamy and unearthly sounds Luigi's
violin—bar after bar of the music monotonous
and sad.   Then of a sudden it wakes to fresh
life with a sort of expression of keen surprise,
and the young man raises his head from the
work that interests him no more, and the
door of his poor dwelling opens.   A few bars
of that haunting melody, that has caused me
to whisper, ' This is love,' merge into a strain
of plaintive hopelessness, and the fair girl
enters.   She is closely veiled, and enveloped
in a long dark cloak, and as she raises the
veil from her face, and looks at him with sad
and wistful eyes, the man's heart responds to
the impassioned strings and vibrates with
love, hopeless though it be.   For I know
that ere two days are past she will wed
another, and the man knows it, and,
crushing down his love, curses her in his
heart for her faithlessness.   He stands for
a moment after her entry helpless in
his surprise at seeing her, and then, with
a grand air of calm politeness, handing

her to one of the crazy chairs that furnished
his poor room, waits, with a cold face, to
learn the object of her visit.   Then the
woman—or the music—pleads in pathetic
strains for pardon and forgiveness—pleads
the pressure put upon her by friends—pleads
her utter helplessness in their hands,—yet
tells him, even with the wedding-ring waiting to encircle her finger, that he alone, the
exiled, poverty-stricken Frenchman, owns
the love her heart can give.   And as the
tears fall from her eyes, the man waves his
arm round the squalid room, and showing by
that gesture his utter poverty and hopelessness, commends, with a bitter sneer, the
course she has taken, or been compelled to
take, and asks how he could expect the
daughter of a noble English family to share
such a home and such a lot as his.   I see
the girl hesitate, falter, and tremble, and as
she rises, the man, with a calm air and forced
composure, opens the door. Weeping bitterly,
she leaves him ; and as he closes the rickety
door upon her, a wail of music, more mournful than words can describe, lingers in the
air, and brings the tears to my eyes, whilst

the man kneels down and kisses the very
boards on which her feet had rested.

With the mirthless smile upon his face, he
sits down thinking, thinking ; and the music,
playing ever, gives me his thoughts.   As I
read them I shudder, knowing how every
fresh departure tends ever and only to the
same end—what has he to do with life any
longer ?—he, the last descendant of a noble
French family, his sovereign an exile, his lands
and possessions confiscated or squandered,
and now he lies starving, or soon to be starving, in a London attic.   Even the fame that
he once hoped to win as a musician is far off;
and, if ever to be won, is it worth struggling
for ?   The past, to him, is full of agonizing
recollections of relatives and friends whose
blood has slaked the guillotine's thirst.   The
present is misery.   The future, now that the
dream of love he had dared for a while to
dream is dispelled, hopeless—what, indeed,
has he to do with life any longer ?   If he
knows not how to live, at least he knows
how to die.

Ever with the same dreary thoughts in his
mind, I see him take the bulky score—the

result of months, it may be years, of labour—
and deliberately tear sheet after sheet to
pieces, until the floor is littered with the
fragments. And as his action tells me he
renounces hope, love, and fame, I know I am
fated to see an awful sight, but am powerless
to move my eyes from the scene. For still
the melancholy notes sound; and I know
that until Luigi's hands are at rest, I am
fettered by the spell the music weaves. I
watch the man, or the phantom, with concen-
trated interest. The last page of the score
falls in tatters to the ground, and, still seated
in the chair which he had placed for the girl,
he stretches out his hand, seeking for something amongst the papers on the table. Well
I know the object he seeks—a small knife,
with an elaborately chased silver handle—a
relic, doubtless, of former riches. To-morrow
even that would have been sold to provide
the bare necessaries of the life he ceases to
care for. He opens it, passes his fingers
across the keen edge, and removing his coat,
turns up his shirt-sleeve to the shoulder, and
deliberately severs a large vein or artery
in his arm. Oh, that maddening music!—

encouraging, tempting, even applauding his
crime of self-destruction! I see, and sicken
at the sight, the first red rush of blood from
his white arm; and then, drip, drip, drip,
follow the large quick-falling drops. So real,
so horrible is the vision, that I can even note
the crimson pool forming amid the tattered
paper covering the floor. Will the fatal
music never end? Minutes are hours as
I watch the face grow whiter and whiter, as
the man sits bleeding to death. Now, whilst
I long to faint and lose the dreadful sight, he
rises, and, with tottering steps, walks across
the room and takes up the violin. With the
life-blood streaming from his left arm, once
more, and for the last time, he makes the
instrument speak; and again, I say, the
music comes from him, and not from Luigi.
As he plays, even whilst I wait for what
must follow, I know that such rare music was
never heard on earth as the strain to which I
listen—fancying the while I can see the eager
wings of Death hovering around the player.
To what can I compare it? A poet would
term it the death-song of the swan. It is the
death-song of a genius—one whom the world

never knew—whose own rash act has extinguished the sacred flame.   Strong and wild
and wonderful rises the music for a while.
Now it sinks lower, lower, and lower.   Now
it is so soft I can scarcely hear it; it is
ebbing to silence, even as the heart's-blood is
ebbing to death.   The face grows ghastly;
the head sinks upon the breast; the eyes
flicker like the dying flame of a candle; the
violin drops from the reddened hand, and the
man falls sideways from his chair to the
ground, even as Luigi's violin completes the
bar his fall had broken off in the middle; and
as it sums up the tragedy in one long-sus-
tained passage of hopeless grief, I see the
bloodless, white face of the man, now dead,
or soon to be dead, lying on the ruddy floor;
whilst the left arm, motionless now, rests as
it had fallen across the violin, which those
nerveless fingers had at last been fain to
drop.

The music stopped—the spell was ended.
So powerfully was I wrought upon by the last
vision I had seen, that the moment my limbs
resumed their freedom, I rushed forward and
fell fainting on the very spot on which it

seemed to me the man had died. When I
recovered consciousness, I found Luigi bending over me, and sponging my face with cold
water. He was pale and agitated, and
seemed from physical exhaustion scarcely
able to stand. I rose, and with a shudder
looked towards that part of the room where
the phantasmagoria had appeared. Nothing
was there now to move me. The familiar wall-
paper, the pictures I had so often scanned,
alone met my eye. As I gazed round, Luigi,
in a whisper, asked :

'You saw it all, then, as I did ?'

'I saw it all: could it have been a dream ?'

He shook his head. 'If so, three times
have I dreamed it, and each time alike in
every detail. The first time I said, " It must
be a dream ;" the second time, " It may be
fancy." But what can I say now, when
another sees it also ?'

I could give him no answer—I could offer
no explanation—only I asked :

'Why did you not cease playing, and spare
me that last sight ?'

'I could not. It was your impulse to play
on that violin, when first you saw it, that led

me to think its strange power would act on another besides myself, and induced me to go through it all once more. But it will tell its story to no one else.'

I turned inquiringly, and seeing on the carpet a mass of small splinters of wood, mixed with tangled strings and pegs, knew what he meant. This, then, was the end of the masterpiece of Stradivarius.

'And you mean to say you had no power to cease when once you began ?—were compelled to play through the whole tragedy ?'

'I had no power to stop. Some force irresistible compelled me. I was but an instrument ; and absurd as it seems, I believe that you, with no knowledge of the art, would have played just as I did.'

'But the music ?' I asked. 'The wonderful music ?'

'That to me,' replied Luigi, 'is the strangest thing of all. Neither you nor I can recall a single bar of it. Even those two or three melodies which, as we heard them, we thought would haunt us, have vanished.'

And it was so. Try how I would, I could fashion no tune at all like them.

'It bears out what I told you,' said Luigi,
in conclusion. 'I was simply an instrument.
Indeed, it seemed the whole time not I, but
another was playing. But here is an end of
it.'

Then, late as the hour was, we kindled a
small fire, and consumed every atom of the
violin which held, in some mysterious, inexplicable way, the story of a man's love and
death.

We parted at last. Luigi left England as
arranged, and has not yet revisited it.

*   *   *   *   *

Is there any sequel to my incredible story?
None that will throw any light upon it, or
enable me—as, indeed, I have little hope of
doing — to win the reader's belief. Only,
some time afterwards, I saw in the house of
a man—known by name at least to all who
are familiar with the titles of the great ones
of the land—the portrait of a lady. It was
that of his mother, who had died a few years
after her marriage ; and if the painter's skill
had not erred, it was also the portrait of the
phantom-woman whom I had seen twice that

night in the visions brought before me by the weird music. Every feature was so stamped upon my memory, that I could not be mistaken. And yet I did not trouble to inquire into her private history. Even if I could have learnt it, it could have told me no more than I knew already. The story of her love and its tragic ending—doubtless a sealed page in her life— had been fully revealed to me as I lay in Luigi's room listening to the varying strains of the haunted Stradivarius.

FLEURETTE.

CHAPTER I.

I HAD spent some years in the colonies, doctoring diggers and the like rough-and-ready folks. The novelty of the strange scenes and free-and-easy life had at last worn off, and I found myself sighing for the respectability of broadcloth and a settled position in my profession. Aided somewhat by thrift, and more by a fortunate land speculation, I had made money enough to supply my wants for a few years to come; so I returned to England, resolved to beat out a practice somewhere.

Of course, the first person I went to see was John. He was my brother—my only brother — indeed, the one tie I had to England. We were a couple of orphans,

but pretty sturdy ones withal, and well able
to wrestle with the world. Fortunately, our
father lived until his eldest son was of an
age to carry on his snug country practice ; so
John still occupied the old red-brick house in
the main street of the little town of Dalebury,
the same brass plate on the door doing duty
for him as for his father before him.

I found old John—so his closest friends
ever called him—little changed : rather
graver in mien, perhaps, but with the same
honest eyes and kindly smile, winning at
once the confidence, and soon the love, of
men and women. As we clasped hands and
looked in each other's faces, we knew that
the years which had made men of us had
only deepened our boyish love.

It was pleasant, very pleasant, for a wanderer like myself to find such a welcome awaiting him. It was good to sit once more in that
cosy old room and talk with John late into the
night, discussing all that had happened since
last we sat there. I had many questions to
ask. Dalebury is only a little town. Having
been born and bred there, I knew all the inhabitants. I had not been abroad long

enough to forget old friends, so I plied John
with many inquiries as to the fate of one or
another.   After a while I asked :

'Who lives now in the old house at the
corner—where the Tanners lived once ?'

'A widow lady and her daughter, named
Dorvaux.'

'French, I suppose, from the name ?'

'No, I believe not.   Her late husband
was French ; but so far as I have learned,
Mrs. Dorvaux is an Englishwoman.'

'New-comers!   They must be quite an
acquisition to Dalebury.   Are they pleasant
people ?'

'I don't know—at least, I only know the
daughter.   She is very beautiful,' added
John, with something very much like a sigh.

My quick ears caught the suspicious sound.
Could I be on the eve of an interesting discovery ?

'Very beautiful, is she ?   And what may
her Christian name be ?'

'Fleurette—Fleurette,' replied John, repeating the soft French name, and lingering
upon it as though it were sweet to his lips,
like wine.

Then he changed the conversation, and far away we drifted from beautiful maidens and musical names, as I recounted some of my colonial exploits—how I had treated strange accidents, out-of-the-way diseases, ghastly gunshot wounds; until our talk became purely professional, and without cheerfulness or interest for the laity.

I spent the next day in looking up old friends and neighbours. I had brought money back with me—not very much, it is true, but rumour had been kind enough to magnify the amount, so every one was glad to see me. Mind, I don't say this cynically; I only mean that, leaving the nuisance of appeals to the pocket, for old sake's sake, out of the question, all must feel greater pleasure at seeing a rolling-stone come back fairly coated with moss than scraped bare. So all my old friends made much of me, and I wondered why the world in general should be accused of forgetfulness.

Whilst I was at one house, another visitor entered, and I was introduced to Miss Dorvaux. As I heard her name, the recollection of my grave brother's midnight sigh

made me look at her intently and curiously ;
more so, I fear, than politeness allowed.

Now you must decide for yourself as to
whether Fleurette Dorvaux was beautiful.
When I say, candidly, that only one person in
the world admires her more than I do, that only
one person is her more devoted slave than I
am, I confess myself a partial witness, whose
testimony carries little weight. But to my
eyes, that day, Fleurette appeared as follows.
About twenty years of age ; scarcely middle
height, but with a dainty, rounded figure ;
brunette, with dark-brown eyes, long black
lashes, making those eyes look darker—such
black eyebrows and such black hair ! nose,
mouth, and chin as perfect as could be :
such a bright, bonny, lively little woman !
Not, I decided at first, the wife for a hard-
working, sober doctor like John Penn.

Stay—is the girl so bright, so lively, after
all ? On her entry she had greeted my
friends with a gay laugh and merry words,
emphasised with vivacious little French
gestures, and for a few minutes she was all
life and sunshine. She seemed interested
when she heard my name, and with easy

grace began talking to me thoughtfully and sensibly. As she talked, something in her manner told me that life was not all sweetness to her. At times her bright brown eyes looked even grave and serious, and the smile, ever on her lips as she spoke, softened to a pensive one. The first impression she made on me, the idea that she was only a brilliant little butterfly thing, left me, and I hastened to atone mentally for the wrong I had done her by saying to myself, 'I am for once mistaken; the girl has plenty of sense, and, likely enough, will and purpose in that pretty head of hers.' However, grave or gay, wise or foolish, I saw in Fleurette Dorvaux a beautiful girl, and pictured woe for many a youth in Dalebury.

After John had seen the last of his patients that night, he joined me in the old room, and with a bottle of good wine between us, I said :

'I saw your beautiful Miss Dorvaux to-day.'

John started as he heard her name, but made no reply ; so I determined to learn all that was to be learned.

It was a very easy task. Old John had never yet been able to keep a secret from me—it may be he never meant to keep this. Anyway, in a short time I heard the whole history of his love.

Fleurette and her mother came to Dalebury some twelve months ago, and John, whose heart had been proof against all local charms, had at once surrendered. There was something in the girl so different from all others. Her beauty, her gracefulness, even her pretty little foreign ways, had taken him by storm; and, so far as I can judge from the symptoms he described, his case was very soon as desperate as that of a boy of twenty. It may be, the very strength of the constitution which had so long defied love made the fever rage more fiercely. Yet, severe as the attack was, the cure seemed easy enough. He had a comfortable home and a good income to be shared; so he set to work seriously to win Fleurette's love. All seemed going on as well as could be wished; the girl appeared happy in his society, and, if she showed him no tangible marks of preference, pleased and flattered by

his attentions. Yet at last, when he asked
her to be his wife, she refused him—sweetly
and sadly, it is true, but nevertheless firmly
refused him.

Now, although I, being four years younger,
and, moreover, his brother, choose to laugh
at John—call him grave, sober and old—you
must understand this is all in jest and by way
of good-fellowship, and that John Penn was
a man whom any girl should have been
proud of winning. He was no hero, or
genius, or anything of that sort; but then
most of us move among ordinary men and
women, and only know heroes, heroines, and
geniuses, as we know princes and dukes—
by name. He was a clever, hard-working
doctor, with a good provincial practice.
Modesty deters me from saying much about
his personal appearance, as the world sees
a strong likeness between us. I will only
say he was tall and well-built, and carried in
his face a certain look of power, which right-
minded women like to see with men who
seek their love. His age was something
over thirty. Our family was good and our
name unsullied. What could have induced

4—2

Fleurette Dorvaux to reject him ? Beautiful
she might be ; but the times are mercenary,
and beautiful girls don't win the love of
a man like John every day in the week.

Although John told me all about it in
a cynical sort of way—a way which sat upon
him as badly as another man's coat might
have done, he could not conceal from me
how deeply wounded he was—how disappointed—or how intense had been his
love for the girl. As he finished his recital
I grasped his hand, saying, with the assur-
ance of one who has seen much life :

' Hard work is the best antidote, and you
seem to have plenty of that—you will forget
all about it in time, old fellow.'

' I don't think I shall. I feel like a man
who, having been kept in twilight all his
life, is shown the sun for an hour, and then
again put back into twilight. He will forget
the sun no more than I shall forget
Fleurette.'

' She seemed to me such a sweet girl,' I
said doubtfully.

' She is perfect,' said John. ' You have
seen nothing of her as yet. Wait until you

can fathom the depths of thought and feeling under that bright exterior. Then you will say I was not wrong in loving her as I did—as I do even now.'

'Has any one else won her? Was that the reason she refused you?'

'No one. She loves me, and me only.'

'What do you mean?' I asked, greatly surprised.

'That evening when she told me firmly and decisively she would never marry me— never could marry me—even whilst I said mad cruel words to her, I saw love in her tearful eyes. And when, forgetting all, I held her and kissed her once, and once only, I felt her lips linger on mine. Then she broke away and fled; but I know such a woman as Fleurette Dorvaux would not suffer a man's kiss unless she loved him. She wrote me a few lines the next day, telling me it could not be, begging me not even to ask her why. Since then she shuns me, and all is at an end; so please talk no more about it.'

Here was a nice complication! Here was a knot to untie! John refused by a girl who loved him! I own I was glad to hear him assert his belief in her love, as, somehow, it pained me to think of Fleurette sporting with a man's heart. Although, as I told you, I determined at first that she was not the right wife for John, I had soon recanted, and thought now how wonderfully she would light up the old house, and how happy John would be with such a bright little woman to greet him when he returned of an evening weary and fagged.

So I resolved to see all I could of Fleurette : to study her, and if I found her as good as John said she was, to use my skill in untying the knot and smoothing the strands of their lives. I never doubted my ability to arrange the matter. I had always been an able family diplomatist. Had I not, at New Durham, brought Roaring Tom Mayne back to his faithful but deserted wife, and seen them begin life together again with courage and contentment? Had I not made those two old friends and partners—who for some time had been prowling about with revolvers in their pockets, hoping to get a snap shot at each other—shake hands, and eventually left them working a new claim together? Had

I not stopped pretty Polly Smith from running away with that scamp Dick Long, who
had two or three wives already, somewhere
up country? In fact, so successful had I
been in arranging other people's affairs, that
it seemed, to an experienced hand like myself,
an easy matter to place John and Fleurette
on a proper footing.

Dalebury is a very little town. Its enemies
even call it a village; but, boasting as it does
of a mayor and a corporation, it can afford to
treat their sneers with contempt. Different
people may hold different opinions as to
whether life is pleasanter in large cities or
small towns; but at any rate, one advantage
offered by a small place like Dalebury is, that
everybody knows everything about everyone
else. You cannot hide a farthing rushlight
under a bushel. So if anybody has anything
to keep secret, don't let him pitch his tent in
Dalebury.

With the universal knowledge of one's
neighbours' affairs pervading the Dalebury
atmosphere, it is not strange that the first
person I chose to ask hastened to give me all
the information respecting the Dorvaux that

Dalebury had as yet been able to acquire.
Mrs. Dorvaux was a widow ; not rich, but,
it was supposed, fairly well off: she was a
great invalid, and rarely or ever went out.
Appearing to dislike society, she received no
one, and scarcely anyone knew her. Those
with whom she had been brought in contact
stated she was a quiet, ladylike woman, who
spoke very little. It was not known whence
they had come—probably France ; but this
was only conjecture, and the absence of cer-
tainty on this point rather distressed Dalebury. They kept only one servant, an old
woman, who had been with them many years.
Fleurette had made many friends, and, it
seemed, few, if any, enemies. She did not
go out much, being devoted to her invalid
mother ; but everyone was glad of her company when she chose to give it. Altogether,
Dalebury had nothing to say against the new-
comers—a fact speaking volumes in their
favour.

After this, as we were such near neighbours, I used frequently to encounter Fleurette, and would often join her and walk with
her. Whether she knew that John's secret

was mine I could not say, but she met my
friendly advances half-way. The more I saw
of her, the more I wondered how I could
have thought her so lively and gay. Whatever she might seem to others, there was, to
me at least, a vein of thoughtful sadness in
the girl's character—at times I fancied it
even approached to despondency; and I felt
almost angry with her, knowing that a turn
of her finger would bring one of the best
fellows in England to her feet. We met old
John once or twice as we were walking together. Fleurette cast down her long lashes
and simply bowed.

'Of course you know my brother well?' I
said.

'I have often met him,' answered Fleurette
calmly.

'And you like him, I hope?'

'I like Dr. Penn very much,' she replied
simply.

'He is the best fellow and the best brother
in the world,' I said; and then I told Fleurette what we had been to each other as boys:
how John had been as careful of me as the
mother who was dead might have been—how

we loved each other now; and as I spoke,
I saw a blush on her clear brown cheek, and
although she said nothing, her eyes when they
next met mine were wistful and kind.

'I shall soon make it all right,' I thought,
as I noted her look, and resolved to argue
the matter on the first fitting occasion.

There is a little river—a tributary to a large
one—running through Dalebury. Being too
shallow for navigation, it is not of much use
except as a water-supply and for angling.
Still, one who knows it can get a boat with a
light draught a long way up. One afternoon,
thinking a little exercise would do me good,
I procured such a boat, and started to row
up as far as I could, and drift leisurely back
with the current. For some distance on one
side of the stream are rich fertile meadows;
and the path along the bank, through these
meadows, is a favourite walk with the Dalebury folk.

As I paddled my boat up the stream,
guiding its course by the old landmarks—
which came fresh to my memory as though I
were a boy yet—and startling the water-rats,
descendants of those amongst whom John

and I made such havoc years ago, I saw in
front of me on the river-bank the dainty little
figure of Fleurette. As I looked at her over
my shoulder, I could see she was walking
slowly, with her head bent down, as one in
thought. 'Thinking of John and her own
folly, perhaps,' I said. So preoccupied was
she, that the sound of my oars did not attract
her attention until I was close to her. Then,
seeing who it was, she waited whilst I rowed
to the bank on which she stood.

'Good-afternoon, Miss Dorvaux,' I said;
'if you will step into my boat, I will row you
as far as the shallows will let me, and then
back home.'

Fleurette hesitated.

'Thank you, Mr. Penn; I think I prefer
strolling along the river-bank.'

'In that case I shall tie my boat to this
willow-stump, and, with your permission, walk
with you. But you had far better come with
me : the boat is quite safe, and I have not
forgotten my cunning.'

'I am not afraid of that,' said the girl,
stepping lightly into the stern of the boat ;
whilst I thought, 'Here is the chance to

reason and expostulate,' and in my conceit felt certain that my arguments would let me bring Fleurette back ready to accept her fate. Well, pride goeth before a fall !

Yet for a while I said nothing to my companion. I did not even look at her. Poor little Fleurette ! I saw, as soon as we met, that tears were on those dark lashes. The smile on her lip belied them, but the tears were there, nevertheless. So I waited for them to disappear before I talked to her, although I half suspected my words might bring others to replace the vanishing drops.

Presently Fleurette cried, in a voice of pleasure :

' There are some water-lilies ! Can we get them ?'

With some trouble I got the boat near them, and Fleurette gathered three or four. As she sat opening the white cups and spreading out the starry blooms, I said :

' Why are you always so sad, Miss Dorvaux ?'

' Am I sad ? Very few people in Dalebury give me credit for that, I fancy.'

' My eyes look deeper down than the

Dalebury eyes.   To me you are always sad.
Why is it ?   You have youth, beauty, and, if
you wished it, could have love.   Why is it ?'

Fleurette turned her eyes to mine.

' Do you think these pale lilies have any
hidden troubles, Mr. Penn ?'

' None, I should say.   They toil not,
neither do they spin, you know.'

' The people who toil and spin are not the
only ones who are unhappy in the world,'
said Fleurette softly.

' Nor are the water-lilies the only flowers
that shut up their hearts, and only open them
after great persuasion.'

She placed one of the white stars in her
dark hair, and said :

'We are getting quite poetical this afternoon.   Was that a kingfisher flew by ?'

Of course, it was no more a kingfisher than
it was an ostrich ; and as Fleurette was now
my prisoner in mid-stream, I was not going
to let her escape or evade my questions for
any bird that flew.

I steadied the boat with an occasional dip
of the oars, and looking her full in the face,
asked :

'Fleurette, why do you treat John so strangely ?'

Her eyes dropped.

' I scarcely understand you,' she said.

'You understand fully.   Why did you refuse to marry him ?'

'I might plead a woman's privilege. If we cannot choose, we can at least decline to be the choice of any particular man.'

'You might plead it if you did not love him ; but you will not plead it, Fleurette.   It is because I know you love him that I ask you for an answer to my question.'

Her fingers toyed nervously with her lilies, but she said nothing.

'If I thought you did not care for him —if you can tell me so—my question is answered, and I am satisfied.   Answer me, Fleurette.'

She raised her head, and I saw her brave brown eyes shining through her tears.

' The proudest day in my life was when John Penn asked me to be his wife—the happiest day would be the day I married him, and that will be—never.'

' Never, Fleurette ?'

' Never—never—never ! Unless——'

Here the girl gave a sort of shudder, and covered her eyes with her hands.

'Tell me what obstacle there can be,' I said gently.

' I cannot. I will not. If I could not tell John, why should I tell you ?'

' Your mother is a great invalid, is she not?' I asked, after a pause.

' Yes,' replied Fleurette.

' Is it possible you fear that John would wish you to leave her ? Is that the reason, Fleurette ?'

' I will tell you nothing,' she said firmly. ' Put me ashore, please.'

' Very well, Miss Fleurette,' I said, resting on my oars. ' Then I give you fair warning, I shall never cease until I find out everything.'

The girl's face flushed with anger.

' What right have you,' she cried, ' to attempt to pry into my private life ? I hate you ! Put me ashore at once.'

Fleurette not only had a will, but a temper of her own.

' I will not,' I said, ' until you give me

some message I can take to John—some word that will let him live on hope, at least.'

'Will you put me ashore?' said Fleurette, stamping her foot.

My only answer was a stroke of the oars, which sent the boat some yards further up the stream.

'Then I shall go myself,' said Fleurette; and before I could comprehend her meaning, she simply slipped overboard, and in a couple of seconds was standing on the river-bank, with the water dripping from her petticoats. She darted across the meadow without even looking back, and left me feeling supremely ridiculous. The river was scarcely knee-deep at this point, so she ran no risk of drowning, and only suffered the inconvenience of wet shoes and skirts; but I could not divest myself of the idea that had there been six feet of water there, the beautiful little vixen would have gone overboard just the same. I had been completely outwitted by a girl of twenty—but then no one could have imagined that a young lady of the present day, attired in an elegant walking-dress, would jump out of a boat to avoid his society, however angry

she might be. Yet I felt very foolish as I
drifted back to Dalebury, and doubted
much if I had done John's cause any
good.

'After all,' I said, 'perhaps my boasted
tact and diplomacy only pass muster in the
free-and-easy community of New Durham,
and I shall be a failure in England. I
had better take the first steamer and go back
again.'

I met Fleurette in the road the next morning. Her face wore a demure smile.

'You treated me shamefully,' I said.

'I should be the one to complain, I think.
The idea of attempting to keep me against
my will! My boots were spoiled; I was
made most uncomfortable, and had to explain
my draggled appearance as best I could.'

'But fancy my horror when you stepped
out of the boat, and picture what a fool I
have felt ever since! Nevertheless, I forgive you,' I said magnanimously.

'And I forgive you,' said Fleurette, with
deep meaning in her voice.

So we shook hands, and renewed our
compact of friendship.

I had now been at Dalebury nearly a month, and purposed, whilst I had time to spare, to make a little trip to the Continent. I intended to stay there two months, then return and begin work. A few days before I left Dalebury, I heard that some one was ill at the house at the corner ; and, with the remembrance of Fleurette's wet shoes and stockings before me, I was very uneasy. However, we soon ascertained that Mrs. Dorvaux was the sufferer, and that Dr. Bush, from the other end of the town, had been called in. I knew this was very annoying to John, as Dr. Bush and he were not the best of friends. In his professional capacity John would, I believe, have attended Fleurette herself without show of emotion ; so why not Fleurette's mother ? Nothing, of course, could be said, as we live in a free country, and people may employ what doctor they choose.

Evidently Mrs. Dorvaux's illness was not of long duration, for I soon saw Fleurette about again. She looked pale and worn, probably from watching and nursing her mother. My holiday at Dalebury had now

run down to its last dregs, so when we met
it was to say good-bye.

'Can it never be, Fleurette?' I whispered,
as our hands clasped before parting.

'Never,' she replied—'never. Good-bye
—good-bye.'

Poor old John! poor little Fleurette!
What mystery was it that stayed the happiness of these two?

I returned home from my travels, tired of
idleness. Having heard of an opening that
promised well, I ran down to Dalebury to
consult my brother. John and I were very
bad correspondents, so I had no news of the
little town since I sojourned there. As I
passed the house at the corner I saw it was
void.

'They have left,' said John, as I eagerly
asked the reason.

'Left! Where have they gone to?'

'No one knows,' said John sadly.
'Shortly after you went abroad, common
rumour said they were thinking of quitting;
and last month they did go.'

'Did she leave no word—no message for
you?'

'Only this,' replied John, opening a drawer in front of him, in which he kept a variety of cheerful-looking instruments. 'I found this one morning on the seat of my carriage. I suppose she threw it in.'

A single flower, the stem passed through a piece of paper with the word 'Adieu' pencilled on it.

Sorry as I was to hear the news, I could scarcely help smiling as John replaced the flower in the drawer. It seemed almost bathos, that little rose, tossed into a doctor's carriage, and now lying amongst old lancets, forceps, and other surgical instruments.

The weeks, the months, even the years, passed by, and we heard nothing of Fleurette. The flower, doubtless still lying in the drawer, was all that was left of old John's little romance.

CHAPTER II.

THREE years soon went by. I was still in England. I had purchased a share in a London practice, and although I found much drudgery in my work, it was a paying practice, and one which would eventually be entirely mine, as my partner, who was grow-ing old and rich, talked of retiring.

Once or twice in every year I had been down to Dalebury. All was the same there. John was still unmarried; and if he said nothing about her, I knew he had not for-gotten the dainty little girl who had rejected his love. Yet not a word had Fleurette sent him. She might be dead or married, for all we knew. I used often to wonder whether I should ever meet her again—whether I should ever learn her secret trouble: for I felt that Fleurette's sadness was not so much from having to give up the hope of being John's wife, as from the cause that compelled her to take that step. I could only hope, and say a word now and then to encourage John to hope also.

One day, whilst snatching a hasty lunch, I was informed that I was wanted at once. I found a respectable servant waiting for me.

'Please to come to my mistress at once, sir,' she said. 'She is taken very ill, all of a sudden.'

'Where does she live ?' I asked. The
servant named a street within a short distance, and in a few minutes I was at the
house.

It was in that description of street which
we term respectable—dull, quiet, and respectable—small houses on each side, letting
at low rents ; rents, most likely, decreasing
as an old tenant left and a new tenant came
in : the sort of place where the falling gentleman and the rising clerk or workman meet
in their downward and upward course. On
our way I asked the servant what had
happened to her mistress.

'I found her sitting in her chair, sir, looking so wild and talking such gibberish, that I
came for you as fast as I could.'

She led the way to a sitting-room. 'Mistress was in there when I left; will you please
go in, sir ?'

I went in, but no mistress was visible. I
saw, with a quick glance, that the room
was prettily furnished—many little feminine
knick-knacks lying about. Hanging to an
easel near the window were two dead birds,
a goldfinch, and a bullfinch, and on the

easel stood a China plate, painted with a faithful representation of the models.

' Decayed gentlefolks,' I said to myself, as the servant's voice, calling me from above, put an end to all further speculations. There was evident alarm in the girl's accents; so I hastened upstairs, and just inside the door of a bedroom saw a woman lying on the floor, either dead or insensible.

With the servant's assistance I lifted her up and placed her on the bed; then proceeded to ascertain what was the matter. It needed, alas! very little professional skill to determine the primary cause of her illness.

I had before me one of those sad cases, unfortunately becoming more and more common, of drunkenness in one whose education and station in life should have raised her far above such a vice. There was no doubt about it. Even if the odour of the woman's breath had not told me the truth, I had seen too many drunken women in my time to be deceived. I could do little to relieve her, then; and after assuring the frightened servant that her mistress was in no danger, I placed her comfortably on the bed, and gave

the girl instructions to loosen her clothes.
As she did so, I looked with pity and some
curiosity on the unhappy woman.

She was a lady, evidently—so far as the
common sense of the word reaches—delicately nurtured and well dressed.   Her
features were pleasing, regular, and refined,
yet, in spite of all this, she lay here a victim
to the same vice that urges the brutal collier
to pound his wife to death, and causes the
starving charwoman to overlie her wretched
baby.

I did not like to expose her weakness to
her own servant, so promised to send round
some medicine, and to look in again in the
evening.

As I stood with the door half open, and
turned to give the servant some last instructions, a girl passed by me hastily, not even
seeming aware of my presence.   Before I
had time to speak, or even to look at her,
she had thrown herself on her knees beside
the bed, and was weeping bitterly over the
unfortunate woman.   Her face as she knelt
was hidden from me, but I could see her
hair was black, and something in the turn

of her graceful figure struck me as being familiar.

'Oh, my poor mamma! my poor mamma!' she sobbed out. 'What shall I do?—again, again! Oh, poor mamma!'

I drew near and said, 'You need not be alarmed at your mother's illness; she will soon recover.'

The girl rose on hearing my voice. She turned round quickly and looked at me. Lo and behold, she was our long-lost Fleurette!

Fleurette—and, as I could see, even through her sorrow, as beautiful as ever! I advanced with outstretched hands; but the girl drew herself up and waved me aside with the dignity of a diminutive empress.

'And so, as you threatened, you have intruded upon my privacy. Go—I will never speak to you again.'

'Miss Dorvaux,' I answered, almost as angry as herself, 'your servant will tell you how I happen to be here, and you will see it is from no wish to intrude. I am going now, but shall return to see my patient this evening, when I hope, for the sake of old days, you will give me a few minutes' conversation.'

Then, as Fleurette returned weeping to her
mother, I departed, revolving many things in
my mind, as the writers say.

I had found Fleurette at last. Actually
living within a stone's-throw of my door!
Perhaps she had lived there ever since she
left Dalebury.   Now having found her,
what was I to do with her?   I guessed that
I had also fathomed her mystery. You see,
it was only a commonplace, vulgar little mystery after all—a mother's drunkenness the
sum-total of it.   Yet, when I thought of the
girl giving up her love and bright prospects
for the sake of keeping her erring mother's
vice a secret: most likely never complaining
of the sacrifice: wearing to the outer world a
bright face that hid from nearly everyone
the sorrow of her heart, it seemed to me that
our little Fleurette was something very near
a heroine, after all.

My first idea was to telegraph to John and
tell him where to find her; but upon consideration I thought it better to wait until after
our interview in the evening.

I found Fleurette alone. She was very
pale, very sad, very subdued—very different,

indeed, from the angry young woman who
had walked into the river three years ago, or
the unjust tyrant who had ordered me from
her presence that afternoon. My first inquiry
was after her mother. Poor Fleurette coloured
as she told me that lady was now almost con-
valescent, and she did not think I need trouble
to see her again. Then she held out her
hand, and as I took it said :

'Please forgive me for my unjust words
to-day ; but I was so vexed, I scarcely knew
what I said.'

'We are always forgiving each other,
Fleurette. Brothers unto seventy times seven
—why not sisters also?'

Fleurette smiled sadly and hopelessly.

'Tell me, Fleurette,' I said, gently, as I
sat down beside her, 'was this the cause?'

She nodded her pretty head.

'Tell me all about it. How long has it
been going on ? I can be as secret as you.'

And then Fleurette told me. I will not
give her words. They were too loving, too
lenient, and ever framing affectionate excuses.
It was a piteous little tale, even as she told
it—a tale of hope growing stronger every day,

till in one hour it was crushed, as a flower is crushed under foot. Then came penitence, contrition, shame, and the ever recurring vows of amendment. And with them hope sprang afresh and bloomed for a while—only to be cut down as ruthlessly as before. And so on for years, ever the same weary round, and although she told me not, ever the same loving care, the same jealous resolve to shield her mother's sins from the vulgar gaze. It was a hard burden for a girl to bear. For this she gave up the hope of being John's wife. She would not leave her mother to perish, and would not injure John, as she shrewdly feared might be the case if she subjected him to the scandal of having a mother-in-law of Mrs. Dorvaux's disposition living with him. Knowing as I know the delicate susceptibilities of patients in a place like Dalebury, in my heart I thought that Fleurette was right.

'And why did you leave Dalebury?' I asked, when she had finished her recital.

'Mamma was—ill—there; so ill, I was obliged to send for a doctor—and I feared people might learn the cause.'

So that was why Dr. Bush had been called in instead of John.

' Then we came to London,' she continued. ' London is so large, I thought we might hide ourselves here.'

' How often do these—these attacks show themselves?' I asked.

'Sometimes not for months; sometimes twice a month. Oh, do you think she can ever be cured? She has been so good, so good for such a long time! If I had not gone out to-day, this might never have happened. Our poor old servant died some months ago, and I could not trust the new one, or she might have prevented it. Do you think she can be cured?'

I shook my head. I knew too well that when a woman of Mrs. Dorvaux's age has these periodical irresistible cravings after stimulants, the case is wellnigh hopeless. Missionaries, clergymen, and philanthropists tell us pleasing and comforting tales of marvellous reformations, but medical men know the sad truth.

I was so indignant at the sacrifice of a young girl's life, that had I spoken my true

thoughts, I should have said, 'Leave the
brandy-bottle always full, always near at
hand, so that——' Well, I won't be too
hard on Fleurette's mother. She must have
had some good in her, for the girl to have
loved her so.

We had, as yet, said nothing about John.
That was to come.

'Fleurette, I shall write to John to-night.
What shall I tell him?'

Her black eyelashes were now only visible

'What can you tell him? You promised
to guard my secret.'

'I shall, at least, tell him I have found
you, and then he must take his own course.'

'Oh, don't let him come here,' pleaded the
girl. 'I could not bear to see him; and perhaps,' she added, with a faltering voice, 'he
doesn't care to hear anything about me now.'

Ah, Fleurette, Fleurette! after all, on some
points you are only a weak woman.

The next day I begged leave of absence
from my partner and patients, and ran down
to Dalebury to tell John the news.

Yet I had little enough to tell him. I was
in honour bound to guard the girl's secret;

so all I could say was, I had found her again,
that she was as bewitching as ever, and, I
believed, loved him still. I could add that
now I knew the reason why she could not
come to him, and I was compelled to own it
was a weighty one—an obstacle which I could
give no hope would be removed for many years.
He must be content with that; it was all the
news, all the hope, I had to give him.

'Very well,' said John, with a sigh, 'I must
wait. All things come to the man who waits;
so perhaps Fleurette will come to me at last.'

Now that I had found Fleurette, you may
be sure I was not going to lose sight of her
again. I was very grieved to learn that her
mother's circumstances were not so good as
of old. Some rascal who possessed the
widow's confidence had decamped with a
large sum of money. Our Fleurette eked
out their now scanty income by painting on
china, and very cleverly the girl copied the
birds and flowers on the white plates. She
never complained, but to me it was more
than vexatious to think that there was a good
home waiting for her if her mother's faults
would allow her to accept it. Now and again

I would give John tidings of her. He never
sought her, being far too proud to come to
her until she sent for him; and as in the
course of the next twelve months the unhappy Mrs. Dorvaux experienced three or
four relapses, I could see little chance of
John ever getting the message for which he
waited. I begged Fleurette to persuade her
mother to enter a home for inebriates, but
the girl would not even broach the subject to
her; so here was youth drifting away from
John and Fleurette—kept apart for the sake
of a wretched woman, and I was powerless
to mend matters.

*   *   *   *   *

But did John and Fleurette ever marry?
You see, this is not a romance, only a little
tale of real life, and, as such, the only way
out of the deadlock was a sad and prosaic
one—a way for which poor Fleurette could
not even wish. Reformation, I say, as a
medical man, was out of the question.

I hope Fleurette will not read these pages,
in which I am compelled to express my true
feelings by saying that, a short time after a
year had expired, Mrs. Dorvaux was obliging

enough to die. I say 'obliging' advisedly, for sad though it be to think so, her death made three people happy ; indeed, as her life was so miserable to her, it may be I should have said four. Fleurette mourned her sincerely : all her faults were buried in her grave, and left to be forgotten. Two months after her death I wrote to John, bade him come to town, and, without even warning Fleurette, sent him to see her. Then he found that all things do indeed come to the man who can wait—even the love that seemed so hopeless and far away.

I don't think John ever knew, or, unless he reads it here, ever will know, the true reason why Fleurette refused him and shunned him for so long. He knows, from what I told him, that it was a noble, self-sacrificing, and womanly motive led her to reject his love, and is content with knowing this. He feels the subject must be ever painful to his bright little wife, and has never caused her pretty eyes to grow dim by asking for an explanation. There is no sadness now with Fleurette. She lights up that old red-brick house ; she is the life of Dalebury, and, moreover, the one woman against whom Dalebury says little or nothing.

The last time I was down there I rowed Fleurette a long way up the shallow stream. Not only Fleurette, but a couple of children as well—dark-eyed, bonny boys, who chatter in French and English indiscriminately. As we passed the spot where the aquatic escapade took place, I turned with a smile to my sister ; but before I could speak, she said beseechingly :

' Don't, please—don't. Old memories are always sad. The present is happy, the future promises fair—let us forget.'

And as she spoke for a moment I saw the sad eyes of the Fleurette of old days. Old memories are sorrowful—let them die !

A CABINET SECRET.

A STORY.

I MADE Robert Headley's acquaintance in the auction-room. I am an idle man, and, having plenty of time, and occasionally a few pounds to spare, have gradually contracted a love for bric-à-brac, the pursuit of which enables me to kill a good many weary hours, and to hoard up, in the shape of old china, etc., money which otherwise would be frittered away on equally useless but less valuable objects.

Headley and I were among the most regular attendants at Christie's, Sotheby's, and other auction-rooms, and, as during the season of the sales we met somewhere almost daily, our mutual tastes soon led to an acquaintance.

Headley was a tall, gentlemanly man of

6—2

about thirty-eight, and evidently had studied the ceramic art deeply. He put me right on several little matters, and once or twice saved me from buying spurious productions. As the true collector loves nothing better than to show his pet objects to another who understands and appreciates their beauties, it was not long before Headley asked me to pay him a visit for that purpose.

'Come early,' he said; 'then we shall have time to go through the cabinets by daylight. Afterwards I will give you some dinner.'

Headley's house was in a quiet square in a good, if not the most fashionable, part of London. I found my host delighted to see me, and panting to show his treasures. He was a genuine member of that species known as ' the enthusiastic collector,' whose passion for accumulating rarities amounts almost to a mania ; and I am bound to say that his collection was one to be proud of. I should tire the reader, ignorant of those delicate distinctive subtleties dear to a collector's heart, were I to expatiate upon the beauties of his old Dresden, Sèvres, Wedgwood and Bentley, rose-backed Nankin, blue-and-white hawthorn pattern, etc. I admired greatly, and envied more.

The collections were arranged with great taste in suitable cabinets; and among the many choice specimens, I think the one that struck me most was a magnificent old Chelsea tea-set. It occupied the centre of one of the cabinets, with articles of lesser value ranged around it, as though paying homage to its superior worth. Leaving out of the question the beautiful blue and white decoration, the reticulated gilding and the artistic painting, the set was the more valuable from the fact that it was perfect.

Headley seemed pleased at the admiration I expressed, and said, with a smile:

'You, a collector, may not be surprised at hearing that I nearly bartered my happiness to make that set perfect.'

I laughed, thinking he was joking, and replied:

'I don't think I would go quite so far as that; but I am sure my happiness would be greater if I owned it.'

'So would any man's be. Look at the

painting, the gilding, the shape, the colour!
Feel the texture of it,' he added, taking the
teapot from its velvet-lined nest, and fondly
caressing it with his long white fingers ; 'you
or I could tell in the dark it was Chelsea by
the softness of the paste.'

'Where did you get it from ?'

'I had the teapot, sugar-basin, four cups
and saucers first.   They belonged to my
mother, and, as I told you, I was nearly
paying too dearly for the rest of it.   But I
will tell you all about it after dinner, if you
care to hear the story.'

The summer afternoon passed very pleasantly among the old china, and at seven
o'clock we were summoned to the dinner-table.

I was presented to Mrs. Headley, a charming young woman of about twenty-eight.
She gave me a cordial welcome, and the
little dinner went merrily enough.   We were
served on old Oriental plates ; the spoons
and salt-cellars were of the coveted Queen
Anne period, and the glass was rare old
Venetian.   Headley certainly had refined and
expensive tastes, and, it seemed, plenty of
means wherewith to gratify them.

When Mrs. Headley rose she begged us, pleasantly, not to linger too long over the wine, as she was all alone.

'Your husband has promised me the history of the Chelsea set,' I said; 'but, under the circumstances, I shall ask him to be as brief as possible.'

'If he does tell you, Mr. Burke,' she said, laughing, 'I shall never, never forgive him, and it would be impossible for me to look you in the face again.'

'My dear,' said Headley, 'our friend Burke is a collector himself, and can sympathize with my weakness. I should never think of relating it, unless it were to a kindred spirit who will fully enter into my feelings.'

After closing the door upon my fair hostess, I refilled my beautifully tinted glass with Lafitte, and waited, with some curiosity, for the promised recital.

Headley commenced :

'Of course, it is all a joke now, and I can well afford to laugh at it, but when the affair of which I am going to tell you happened, it was serious enough. The portion of the

Chelsea set I owned at first belonged to my
mother; she inherited it from her father, and
there its history is lost. When I was first
seized with the passion for collecting, it
naturally formed the nucleus of my cabinet.
Everyone admired it, and envied me the
possession of it. One day—it was after I
had formed a decent collection and was
getting well known as a buyer—Wharton,
the dealer, called upon me to show me a few
things he had picked up in the country. I
drew his attention to my Chelsea; he
examined it closely, and said : "Very strange;
I saw the rest of that service a few days
ago." I asked him where, and he told me it
belonged to a lady living at Shepherd's Bush.
Was it for sale ? Certainly not, or he would
not have told me about it until he had secured
it. He had offered to give her a large sum
for it, but nothing would induce her to part
with it. It was, like mine, a family relic,
and as the owner was in no want of money,
there did not seem to be any chance of per-
suading her to surrender it. Her name, he
informed me, was Miss Crofton ; her residence,
142, College Road, Shepherd's Bush.

'Now, Burke, you will, I know, sympathize with me when I say that, having discovered that the rest of the exquisite set was in existence, I felt that life was simply intolerable without it, and that at any sacrifice it must be mine. On this point my mind was at once made up.

'The first thing was to see the china, and satisfy myself that Wharton had made no mistake; so the next day I called upon Miss Crofton. I found her a pleasant, polite lady of about fifty, who presented the appearance of a spinster whose circumstances were very comfortable. It has always seemed to me that anything to do with china makes the whole world kin, and when I explained the object of my call, Miss Crofton, refusing to listen to any apology, at once led me to the cabinet which held the treasure. My informant had told the simple truth. I had the teapot, four cups and saucers, and the sugar-basin; whilst Miss Crofton was the fortunate owner of the cream-jug, eight cups and saucers, and the two dishes. And as, with dazzled eyes, I gazed on her portion of that exquisite service, I felt as if a sacred duty had devolved upon me to reunite the long-separated ceramic family ; and I knew I should find little happiness until·all the beautiful members of it reposed safely in my possession.

' Miss Crofton and I soon became good friends, especially when upon comparing notes and tracing back the pedigree of the Chelsea, we decided that at some time my mother's and her father's families must have been closely allied. When we had established this fact to'our satisfaction, I ventured to hint, as delicately as I could, my wish to possess the china; then, as she took no notice of my hints, I was at last compelled to ask her, point blank, if she would sell it to me, fixing any price in reason she chose to. I found, as Wharton predicted, that the good lady was obdurate, and there I sat for an hour, with the coveted articles almost within grasp, yet as far off as the gates of heaven.

' I did not, of course, despair entirely. " I must manœuvre," I thought. " I will have it in time, by fair means or foul. I will make myself very agreeable to her; I will show her attentions. Some day I may be able to render her a service, and her heart may open with gratitude, and I shall compass my desire." To-day I could do no more, so I bade my new-found relative, as I cunningly called her, an affectionate good-bye, asking permission to call on her again.

' " I shall be glad to see you at any time, Mr. Headley," she said ; " but we shall never have any china dealings together, so you are fairly warned."

' I went home feeling very mournful, and for the rest of that day the eight cups and saucers, the cream-jug, and the two dishes were dancing about before my eyes. I sat down for an hour or more with my own portion before me. How meagre it looked now! I took the pieces out and re-arranged the cabinet, leaving blank spaces for those I coveted. I pictured the lovely appearance the set would present, when the whole of it was in my hands.

' I went to rest quite sorrowful, and the cabinet, which only the morning before seemed so well filled, was now empty, or nearly empty, in my eyes. It is a small thing to say that I believe I dreamt of Miss Crofton and her china the whole night. My honesty vanished as my eyes closed. I stole that china at least a dozen times. I secreted it in the most extraordinary places. I buried it for safety and to avoid detection, but the eight cups seemed endowed with life, and as fast as I covered them up with earth, would pop up in unexpected places. I committed other crimes for the sake of that china. I deliberately murdered the unfortunate spinster, and packed the articles which had urged me to crime most carefully in a bag. Then the hue and cry was raised, and I knew that men were pursuing me, but I dare not venture to run, lest I should break those fragile things for which I had endangered my soul. It seemed to me infinitely preferable to swing on the gallows than to find one of those exquisite cups in atoms. Even when the morning came, and I found that the events of the night were only dreams, my state was not very much happier. I could not bear to look at my cabinet. Something was wanting there, and until that void which my desire had created was properly filled, I felt that I

could find no pleasure in my former pur-
suits.

'You, although a collector, may think I
am joking, but I assure you I am not. I
hungered, I craved for that china, and felt
that, were it denied me, my dreams might
some day almost come true.

'After the interval of a few days, I thought
I might venture to call upon Miss Crofton
once more. She received me kindly, told
me she was flattered by my paying her
another visit so soon, and allowed me to
handle the china again. I must have been
dull company too, for although I replied
mechanically to her chit-chat, my eyes were
ever turning to those eight cups and saucers,
cream-jug and two dishes. Miss Crofton
could see the bent of my thoughts, for she
said :

' " It's no use, Mr. Headley. I will not
sell them, and I love them too much to give
away."

'As she spoke a thought struck me. I
would take her to see the tea-pot, sugar-
basin, and the other cups and saucers,
mourning as it were for their long lost

brethren. So I concealed my vexation, and
making an effort to smile, said :

' " I am only admiring, Miss Crofton.
But I should be so pleased if you would
honour me by calling and looking at my
little collection. If so, I will send the
carriage for you to-morrow."

' She accepted my invitation, and the next
day came to my house. I took care to have
a choice little repast prepared, of such things
as middle-aged spinsters love, and after we
had discussed it I led her to the room which
held my treasures. All the cabinets save
one were open to her view, but that one I
had covered with a dark cloth. After she
had seen the contents of the others, I led
her before this one, and in a theatrical
manner, with a beating heart, lifted the veil
and revealed my tea-pot, sugar-basin, cups
and saucers, looking beautiful, but sorrowful,
with the vacant spaces around them. I said
nothing, thinking this mute appeal to her
better feelings would do more than any words
of mine. She saw the plot at a glance, and
laughed long and loud, saying, as her merriment subsided :

' " So, Mr. Headley, this is the meaning of your hospitality; you expect me to pay for my dinner with the china ?"

' I protested it was only a little hint to show her how very anxious I was to possess the remainder of the set, and then I told her, seriously, how necessary it was to my happiness and peace of mind to see those void spaces filled.

' No appeal of mine would soften her, and the eight cups and saucers, the cream-jug, and the two dishes, seemed as far away as ever. At last she said decisively :

' " As you are so bent upon it, I will bequeath the china to you."

' " And I may have to wait twenty years for it," I said sulkily, forgetting, in my mortification, not only politeness, but the affection I had expressed for my new-found relative.

' " A good deal longer, I hope," she replied. " But as you are so anxious, why not pack up what you have and let me take it back with me ? You can see it all in my cabinet whenever you like ; and I dare say its being there will give me the pleasure of your company more often.'

'But this plan did not suit me at all; and finding that my device had failed utterly, I was obliged to conduct my visitor to her home in a frame of mind not the sweetest.

'A week went by; but, try how I would, I could not get that cursed china out of my head, or resign myself to the disappointment. I found myself growing worse instead of better, and, as I fancied my health was beginning to suffer, I determined to run down to Brighton in the hope of distraction. The weather was fine; I met several pleasant friends there, and, moreover, picked up one or two Wedgwood medallions, the soft soapy feel of which, so aptly compared by Mr. Gladstone to the touch of baby's flesh, was eminently soothing and comforting; and after a day or two I began to think that in time I might conquer the absurd craving for what could not be mine. But even as I was congratulating myself on the partial recovery of my senses, I dreamed a dream so horrible, that I fell back into my former unhealthy state of mind. I dreamed that Miss Crofton's maid—a red-cheeked, rough-fingered lass— had broken two of the cups. I saw her do it ; and suffered agonies from the sight ; also, to make matters worse, I dreamed that she put the precious fragments (which might have been cemented) in her dustpan, with the intention of throwing them away. I really think the greatest feeling of pleasure I had known for many days was to awake and find it was only a dream.

' I hurried back to town the same day. I could endure the uncertainty, the anxiety, no longer, and felt that to obtain my desire, any sacrifice I could make must be made ; so — don't laugh too much — I resolved, upon my return, to ask Miss Crofton to become Mrs. Headley ; and then upon the day of our marriage the severed set would be reunited. True, she must be somewhere about fifty, whilst I was just thirty ; but from what I had seen of her, I believed she was a very worthy woman ; and, anyway, the china would be mine.

' You will scarcely credit it, but I carried out my resolution. Two days later I was at the fair spinster's side, beseeching her to be my wife. I could not bring myself to profess a sudden passion for her ; but I told her I was tired of living alone, and asked her to share my lot. I said I was well-to-do in the world, and promised to try and make her future life a happy one; and as, whilst speaking, my eyes rested on the eight cups and saucers, the cream-jug, and the two dishes, no doubt I pleaded with a show of fervour which must have considerably puzzled the good lady. Like a sensible woman, she expressed the greatest astonishment.

' " Let me understand you clearly," she said. " Do you mean to say you are in love with me ?"

' " I will make you a good husband," I replied, thinking as I spoke how beautifully modelled the handle of the cream-jug was ; " and I am sure you will never regret accepting my offer."

' " But do you really love me ?" she persisted, " an old woman as I am ?"

' " Seventeen hundred and sixty," I said mentally, " that must be about the date it was made ;" and then I answered, looking at the eight cups and saucers, and thinking of the vacant spaces at home : " I esteem and respect you highly, dear Miss Crofton, and I am sure you will make a solitary home cheerful."

' " Suppose," said Miss Crofton acutely, " I were to take the poker and demolish that china, would you still repeat these flattering assurances of affection?"

' "Oh, please don't!" I cried, starting up as the horrors of my dream came back to me.

' " Mr. Headley," she said gravely, " you will pardon me saying so, but sometimes I am afraid you are not quite right in the head. Is there any insanity in your family ?"

' " None at all," I replied.

' " Neither your father, nor mother, neither any aunt nor uncle, shown any tendency that way ?"

' "Not the slightest."

' "Very well ; you had better go home now, and think quietly over what you have said to me. If, to-morrow, you wish to repeat your words, you will find me at home all the after-noon."

' I left her, and as I stepped out congratulated myself that she had not accepted me at once.

' "What a fool I am!" I said. " I shall always esteem that woman for not taking advantage of me. I will write and beg her pardon for my silly conduct, and trust she will still continue my friend." And yet, in spite of these praiseworthy resolutions, the sight of the vacant spaces sent all my good sense to the winds ; and, to shorten the tale, I went deliberately the next afternoon to Shepherd's Bush, renewed my offer, and left the house formally betrothed to Miss Lesbia Crofton. She, at least, behaved in a very sensible manner.

' " You say you wish to marry me," she said, " and I am getting on in years now, so cannot, in justice to myself, refuse such an offer. I have inquired about you, and every-one who knows you speaks in your favour. Still, you may regret your choice, so you shall have plenty of time for consideration. We will not be married for six months, at least."

' Although, after taking the first plunge, I should have been glad to go to the depths of my folly without delay, I felt the wisdom of her words, and acquiesced in this arrange-

ment. Of course, with the new understanding between us, I saw both her and the china
nearly every day ; and as Miss Crofton was
an extremely nice woman, I may say I grew
quite to love her—as a mother—and, had
fate not interposed, should doubtless have
married her at the expiration of the time she
named, and very probably should have been
happy enough, after a fashion.   One thing
was very much to my Lesbia's credit : she
indulged in no raptures, nor did she expect
any from me.   When we met, or parted, I
imprinted a kiss upon her forehead, and that
was all.   She even interdicted the use of
Christian-names between us, and stipulated
that our engagement should be spoken of
to no one.   Another thing I found strange,
was that she was continually harping, in a
good-tempered sort of way, upon the disparity of our ages, instead of endeavouring
to make the difference as little as possible.
In fact, she seemed to treat me more as a son
than as a future husband.

‘ Feelings of delicacy prevented me from
asking her to allow me to remove the Chelsea
to my house before I had paid the price due

for it, and I quite blushed with shame when
one day she handed me the key of the cabinet,
and with a meaning smile begged I would
take charge of it to ensure the safety of the
articles I so highly prized.

'The course of our affection ran very
smoothly for about a month. I had quite
recovered my health, and I may say was
placidly happy. If, at times, whilst sitting
with my elderly bride-elect, and hearing her,
it may be, complain of some ailment which
she candidly attributed to advancing years, I
did feel a twinge of regret, I had but to turn
to the eight cups and saucers, the cream-jug,
and the two dishes, and it vanished.

'But fate and Miss Crofton had other
views for me, although I little suspected it.

'According to custom, one afternoon I paid
my usual visit to my future spouse, and was
surprised as I entered the house to hear
the sound of a piano. I know something of
music, so at once became aware that the
instrument was played with great skill, and
much I wondered who the performer might
be. I had not as yet discovered that my
Lesbia possessed musical talent. The maid

opened the door of the drawing-room, the
music ceased, and I walked in, and found
myself face to face with one of the loveliest
girls I had ever met.

'Perhaps the surprise, the contrast, when I
saw her instead of the middle-aged lady I expected to greet, made this stranger look even
more charming. I could realize only at first
a bright young face, with masses of light hair
around it, turned to see who entered, and a
well-moulded figure, showing to great advantage as she sat before the piano. Her dress
was of simple black, but well and becomingly
made, and as she rose when I entered, I
could see she was over middle height.

'Women always behave with less awkward-
ness than men in chance meetings; so whilst
I stood still and stammered out some words
of apology, she advanced with perfect ease
and said:

'"Mr. Headley, I am sure! My aunt told
me to expect you. She has gone out for a
short time, but hoped you would wait until
her return."

'I was only too pleased to accept the
invitation so frankly given, and recovering

my self-possession, in a few minutes was in full swing of chat with my Lesbia's niece.

' I found her an unaffected girl, full of spirits, and looking forward to the pleasures of a stay in town.

' " I suppose you will stay some time ?" I asked. " Your presence will quite brighten Miss Crofton's house."

' " I shall stay as long as ever my aunt will keep me," she replied. " Isn't she a dear old soul, Mr. Headley ?"

' I winced, and began to realize that my situation was a painful one.

' " She is so antiquated," she continued, "and yet so romantic in many things."

' I felt more foolish than ever, and for the sake of saying something remarked :

' " I wonder she did not tell me you were coming. I suppose she meant to surprise me."

' " I suppose so. But I assure you she has talked to me a great deal about you, Mr. Headley. You appear to be great friends. Quite a flirtation, I tell her."

' I coloured up to my ears, but managed to say :

' " Then I conclude her report of me has been favourable."

' " I shan't betray her confidence, Mr. Headley; and, anyway, it would have no weight with me, as I prefer to form my own opinions."

' As I felt we were getting on delicate ground, I begged her to resume the music which my coming had cut short.

' She played a piece of Chopin's with great feeling and brilliancy, and then, at my request, sang a couple of ballads. Her voice was sweet and well trained—altogether she was a very charming niece-to-be.

' " Do you play or sing ?" she asked.

' " Neither, unfortunately. I am but an indifferent critic, who understands music only enough to praise when pleased."

' " Ah, I forgot ; you are a great china collector."

' And as she spoke, it struck me that this was the first time I had ever been inside this room, and neglected to look and assure myself of the safety and well-being of the cups, saucers, cream-jug, and dishes.

' And as the thought of the china brought

other thoughts in its train, I felt that I would
give a great deal to know whether Miss
Crofton had told her niece everything. Fer-
vently I hoped that she had not done so, as
I knew intuitively I should cut a sorry figure
in a young girl's eyes.

'During my meditation Lesbia returned,
and instead of appearing jealous and annoyed
at the capital understanding between the fair
niece and future uncle, smiled and said :

'"Shall I introduce you young people, or
have you dispensed with that ceremony ?"

'"Your niece has the advantage of me in
knowing my name," I replied.

'"Mr. Robert Headley, let me present
you to Miss Ethel Crofton, my favourite
niece," said Lesbia, with the politeness of the
old school.

'"After that unnecessary ceremony I shall
go and dress for dinner," said Miss Ethel
Crofton.

'I closed the door after her, and turned to
greet her aunt with the accustomed salute.
Perhaps from the same reason that the china
had lost its charm to-day, I found that semi-
maternal affection was scarcely satisfying

enough, and could not help thinking my future bride looked very aged.

' " Robert," she said—it was, I believe, the first time she had used my Christian-name— " I should much prefer that Ethel should hear nothing of our engagement at present. She is young and giddy, and might not look upon it in the right light."

' I promised secrecy with a joy I could scarcely conceal. At any rate, Ethel knew nothing about it as yet.

' I dined that evening with the ladies. Miss Crofton did the honours in a dress of such antiquated design and material that Ethel openly rallied her upon it. She herself was beautiful in pale-blue silk, and I was so struck by her fair, young bright face, her pleasant natural manner, that before the evening was half spent I had fully realized what an ass I had made of myself.

' My visits to Shepherd's Bush, for the next few days, were as frequent as the most exacting *fiancée* could have expected ; but I am afraid that had my Lesbia been of a jealous or suspicious nature she would not have derived the pleasure from them which she appeared to feel. I no longer sat in the chair commanding the best view of the cabinet that enshrined the treasures for which I contemplated sacrificing myself and my affections. I was ever by Ethel's side ; at the piano, turning the leaves of her music ; reading my favourite poems to her ; holding her crewels, or winding wool for her. Considering the tender relations between Miss Crofton and myself, I must own that my behaviour towards her unsuspecting niece was disgraceful. Indeed, had Lesbia thought fit to pour a storm of reproach upon me, and order me to quit her presence, she would have been fully justified. However, she did nothing of the kind, but sat in her favourite corner, knitting, and apparently paying no attention to the flirtation, or something more serious, which was proceeding under her very eyes.

'Soon matters reached a climax. I could no longer deceive myself. I was hopelessly in love with Ethel Crofton, and I felt bound in honour to inform her aunt, and to throw myself on the fair spinster's mercy before I made the avowal of my love to Ethel.

'I found Lesbia alone one day, so I took the little key from my waistcoat pocket and handed it to her.

'"And what is this for, Robert?" she asked gravely.

'In a shamefaced manner I said:

'"I can't marry you—I love Ethel."

'"Oh, Robert—Robert!" said Miss Crofton, putting her handkerchief to her eyes; "what can I say to you? Only a month ago I was indispensable to your future happiness; and yet you forsake me for the first young face you see;" and she appeared to sob bitterly.

'"It was the china," I expostulated.

'"I see; and now you think you can have Ethel and the china too, and prefer a young bride and old china to an old bride and old china. Faithless man!"

'I lost my temper utterly, and I am sorry to say my politeness followed it.

'"Damn the china!" I cried; "give me Ethel, and she can smash it all if she likes. I don't care."

'Women, I believe, under such circumstances as these, like to hear a man swear.

It shows he is in earnest.   Anyway, my deposed bride leant back in her chair, and laughed so heartily that I knew matters would be soon arranged to my satisfaction. In great delight I caught her in my arms, and for once gave her a kiss of real affection.

‘ “ Did you think I was going to let you marry me for the sake of a few cups and saucers ?” she cried.   “ I am not such a stupid old woman as that.   But in truth, Robert, I have grown very fond of you, so if Ethel will have you, take her.   But only on conditions.”

‘ “ Name them, dear Miss Crofton !” I exclaimed ;   “ anything — everything   you wish.”

‘ “ You must prove the earnestness of your love for my darling girl, and your recovery from your temporary insanity, by sending me your Chelsea as a present.   I shall then give the whole set to the South Kensington or Jermyn Street Museum.”

‘ I mustn’t tell you all about our love-making, or Mrs. Headley would never forgive me ; but Ethel and I arranged matters very quickly, and upon my return home that evening, I opened my cabinet, and almost without a pang packed my four cups and saucers, tea-pot, and sugar-basin, in cotton wool, and the next morning forwarded them to Miss Crofton. You have seen Ethel, and I dare say you think I did not make a bad exchange.' Here Headley paused; perhaps he was not sure what a collector would say to his conduct.

'I should think not,' I said. 'But how comes the set to be in your cabinet now?'

'The old lady kept me in great suspense all the time Ethel and I were engaged, and although I hid my feelings, I soon began to think that it would be very nice to have Ethel and the china, but I dared not hint such a thing to Miss Crofton, who, moreover, teased me dreadfully by praising in Ethel's presence my generosity in making her so beautiful a present.

'Whilst on our honeymoon, I thought no more of it—in fact, gave it up for lost; and you may guess my joy when we returned to town, at seeing in my room a strange cabinet with the set as you saw it to-day. So I got a good wife and completed the service as well.'

Just then the door opened, and Mrs. Headley said, with assumed petulance :

'Are you gentlemen ever coming ? Aunt Lesbia is upstairs, Robert, and wishes to see you before her carriage fetches her.'

'Let us go up, Burke,' said Headley, as we finished the last of the claret ; 'and if you want any more particulars of my Chelsea mania, Miss Crofton will give them to you.'

THE BANDSMAN'S STORY.

AT twenty I believed I was sent into the world to become a second Beethoven—at twenty-five I was playing the flügel-horn in a German band, and thought myself lucky in getting that appointment.

It seems a great drop—a fall from the stars to the mire ; but as my own particular fortunes or misfortunes have little bearing upon the events which I am going to relate, I need not dwell upon them at any length. Left an orphan at an early age, bred up in a small village under the care of an old aunt, what wonder that the astonishment caused in the little world around, by the musical talent of which I gave early evidence, quite turned my head ?   The boy who could play upon all and every instrument by ear alone, and,

moreover, play melodies which he really
thought at the time were original, was looked
upon by the simple people about as a heaven-
born genius, and naturally felt averse to
earning a prosaic living by commerce. So
exalted was he, in fact, that having acquired
a smattering of harmony, and, through the
kindness of some old friends, a hundred
pounds to give him a start, he felt little fear
of failure when he resolved to wring fortune,
if not fame, from Music, heavenly maid.

How soon a man finds his level in London!
How soon I found mine! and found, moreover, that within the boundaries of the
United Kingdom there must be at least five
thousand young fellows each with talents
equal to, if not greater than, mine.

Having learnt my lesson, hard as it was,
thoroughly, the next thing was to find out
how to live. My money was at last spent,
and I think my dreams of success fled entirely as I changed the last sovereign ; and
then, almost cap in hand, I was fain to wait
upon those great publishers whom in my
dreams I had patronised, and beg for work,
however humble. So then I became a helot,

a drawer of water and carrier of wood to the
divine mistress, Art.   I copied scores, I
tuned pianos when I could get that task in-
trusted to me ; I gave elementary lessons
when I could find pupils.   It was dreary
work, but somehow for the next few years I
managed to live ; and then, tired of the
ceaseless and unremunerative drudgery, I
sank all pride and donned the gay blue-and-
white uniform of the Upper Rhine Band,
engaged to perform from May to October
at the rising watering-place, Shinglemouth.

It was a hard life, but I believe not an
unhealthy one, if a man could boast a good
constitution, sound limbs and strong lungs.
Being on one's feet the whole day was the
most fatiguing part of it.   It was unpleasant,
also, playing in half a gale of wind, or with
cold drizzling rain falling ; but worse than all
to me were the burning days in July and
August, when the sun glared down upon us
—vicious, it seemed to me, at finding his
dazzling rays reflected from our bright brass
instruments.   Then I confess I looked with
envy upon the holiday folks for whom we
made sweet music, as they sat placidly under

the shade of the trees or their own umbrellas; and I longed to tear off my close-fitting tunic and revel in the green sea at my feet. Yet, in spite of all these drawbacks, after my sedentary life in London, I was contented and comfortable enough.

The Upper Rhine Band was not one of those harrowing little atrocities which go about with five or six ignorant performers, braying on battered brass instruments—re leasing one of their number every ten minutes to go on a begging expedition. We were a properly organized and fairly musical company, engaged and paid by a committee of the townspeople to enhance the natural attractions of Shinglemouth. Far too dignified were we to pass the hat round. If our listeners chose to give, there was a box placed conveniently for that purpose; but as all such vicarious contributions went to the committee's fund, it mattered nothing to us.

Probably the inner life of a German band would be without general interest, so I will only say that our quarters were in a dingy little street at the back of the fine row of new buildings on the Esplanade. We lodged

in twos and threes at various small houses.
We met together at a certain hour in the
morning to commence our rounds, and at
nine o'clock at night our duties were over,
our instruments put into their cases, and
each man his own master—free to smoke,
drink, or go to bed, as he pleased.

Although the name we gave ourselves—
' The Upper Rhine Band '—was intended to
stamp our origin as being Teutonic, there
were several in the company who, like myself, only spoke English ; but as these were
quite as good musicians as their German
comrades, the fraud was a very little one.
My tale concerns no more than two men, so
I need only mention the names of these—
Caspar Hoffman, a German, and Stephen
Slade, an Englishman. The former played
the clarionet—an instrument which, in the
constitution of a German band, takes the
place of the first violin in an orchestra. The
latter played that enormous mass of metal
called a serpent.

Hoffman was a tall, light-haired man : his
age was about thirty. His face was handsome, and bore an expression of great amia-

bility. His manner invited friendship at
once ; and my strange new life seemed easier
and pleasanter to me when this frank young
German chose to discover a kindred spirit in
mine, and insisted upon our lodging and
chumming together. It took me very little
time to find out that he was a man of education and reading, and that his acquirements
were far more than might have been expected
from one in his position. He had lived in
England a long time, and spoke our language
easily, and he told me he was almost as well
acquainted with French. It seemed strange
to me that so well-educated, I might almost
say so accomplished a man, should fill so
lowly a post in the world. Indeed, I began
to weave a little romance about him, fancying
he must be an exiled nobleman or political
offender. When I knew him well enough to
venture to express my wonder, and ask for
an explanation, he laughed a bitter laugh,
saying :

'There is nothing to explain, my friend.
My little history is the history of thousands
of my countrymen. The eldest son of a
small farmer; given an education that

straitened the means of my people; sent out
as certain to find employment and fortune
for myself and all belonging to me in your
great London.

'*Ach!* what find I there? Tens of
thousands of young Germans like myself, all
striving to get into merchants' offices and
make the promised fortunes. Everywhere I
offered myself—not even a pound a-week
could I get. Then I began to starve, and
the consul offered to send me back. How
could I return? Then I found I could make
a living by that gift natural to most of my
countrymen. And now I play the clarionet
till Fortune finds me something better
to do.'

Any way, if not a prince in disguise, my
light-haired German was a fine fellow : a true
friend to me when I most wanted a friend,
and a great favourite with all. Even the
surly toll-taker at the pier gates was civil to
him. The nursery-maids, heedless of their
charges, looked upon him with that open-
mouthed admiration usually reserved for the
military; and, although with trembling I say
it, I have seen ladies whose rank in life

should have forbidden such condescension, glance with approval at his fine face and manly figure. Yet when I said above that he was a favourite with all, I should have made an exception — Stephen Slade, the Englishman.

I knew little of this man, and that little was not pleasing enough to make me wish for a closer acquaintance. I may say, in passing, that I am not a bandsman now. Fortune at last gave the wheel a half-turn, which placed me at least above such struggles for a living. At the time of which I write, I had little enough to be proud of; but, fallen as I was in the world, there were a few men in the band with whom I could scarcely bring myself to associate on intimate terms. This man Slade was one of them.

The son of the poorest parents, his present position was to him as much a rise in the world as it was a fall to Hoffman and myself. Yet he appeared to be a sullen, discontented man. Those who knew him better than I did said he was clever and crafty, but could be pleasant enough company when he chose. I never tried to ascer-

tain the truth of the latter assertion, although
I fully believed the former. I disliked the
man, his appearance, and his ways. He was
broad-shouldered and powerful, although
clumsily and coarsely made. That our dislike was mutual, I knew: indeed, we had
quarrelled about some trivial matter the first
day we met; and ever since, I had studiously
avoided him. I felt that the man was of a
vindictive nature, and would do me an evil
turn if he found the opportunity; but unless
I was foolish enough to be provoked to a
personal encounter, in which his great strength
would be of service to him, I could scarcely
see how he could harm me.

It often pleased him to throw out sneering
remarks about gentlemen and their ways—
intended, of course, for the benefit of Hoffman and myself. Caspar would parry these
attacks with jesting good-humour and ready
wit, oftentimes raising a hearty laugh from
his listeners at the expense of Stephen Slade.
Yet I knew that even if these merry sar-
casms struck well home, it was for another
cause that Slade hated my friend—that
cause which has ever been answerable

for so much bad blood between man and man.

One night, when Caspar and I were sitting in our poor little room, talking together, and finishing our pipes before going to bed, Slade's name was mentioned.

'How that wretch hates you!' I said.

'*So!* hates me?'

'Yes; I can see him glaring sideways at you, even whilst blowing his heart out over his awful instrument.'

'Ah, he is not a pleasant man. Yet I thought it was you he honoured with his dislike, not me.'

'He dislikes me, and would no doubt injure me if he could; but you he hates. I see it in his look.'

'And for what cause?'

'Need we go very far to seek the cause? Certainly not a quarter of a mile.'

Casper laughed, but made no reply.

The cause of Slade's animosity lay very near at hand. Where the corner of our dingy little street went round towards the Esplanade was a second or third rate inn; not an establishment that for a moment

THE BANDSMAN'S STORY. 123

dared to enter into competition with the
great hotels on the Esplanade, but which
nevertheless did a fair and lucrative business
with the rank and file of excursionists to
Shinglemouth. This inn we had to pass
and repass morning, noon, and evening,
going to and coming from the pier. After
our work was over, many of us, when able
to afford it, were glad to pause and drink a
glass of beer or spirits. The inn was kept
by a widow named Deane—a woman reported well-to-do in the world, owning, as
she did, the house, and doing good business
there. Now Mrs. Deane had one daughter,
an only child, and reputed heiress to all her
mother's wealth—wealth that, to the German
members of our fraternity, must have seemed
fabulous—a dower almost large enough for
one of the numerous princesses of Father-
land. This girl, Mary Deane, was really
handsome—dark-eyed, dark-haired, and rich
in colour. She was, I must say, a well-
conducted, virtuous girl, perhaps showing at
times a little of that coquetry which appears
to be inseparable from good looks, when
owned by a girl of her rank in life. As it

seems necessary for their comfort that every body of men should raise up a goddess to adore, Mary Deane, by common consent of our unmarried members at least, was exalted to that proud position ; and the amount of broken but devoted English wafted to her across the shining counter was enough to give the girl ear-ache, if not heart-ache. Of course I ought to have followed my fellows' example, and fallen in love with her ; but somehow — and somehow — in spite of all failures, my dreams had not quite left me, and genius in a white apron drawing beer seemed rather out of the fitness of things. Again, it was not long before I found that my light-haired German, Caspar, was the man on whom the girl had set her heart.

Have I written the above lines in a light vein ? If so, it was far from my intention. As I picture him now, smiling at the girl with that frank open smile of his, and calling up on her face that scarcely disguised look of pleasure, my thoughts are only sad ones. Not for a moment did I think that Caspar was wooing the girl either for her undoubted charms or possible possessions ;

but, like other men I have known, he had, without meaning harm, a dangerous knack of dropping his voice and softening those clear blue eyes of his when speaking to a pretty woman ; and if Mary Deane mistook these symptoms for dawning love, who can blame her ? You must always remember that in social standing, and so far as outside appearances went, there was a great gulf between her and a clarionet-player in a German band, and she stood on the side nearer heaven. Yet when Hoffman entered the house and gave his modest orders, she invariably came out from the little parlour behind to minister to his wants—an act of condescension certainly not accorded to many of our comrades.

Let Caspar be grateful or not for the favours shown him, one other man, at least, would have given much for them ; this was Stephen Slade.

With all his faults, the man was not a drunkard, yet at every leisure moment he haunted the corner house, and in his own unpleasant fashion wooed the girl. First to enter and last to leave, he sat and scowled

at all who interchanged a word with Mary
Deane, till men grew nervous and uncomfortable under his sullen gaze, and the girl
herself could only escape it by taking refuge
in the private sanctum, where no one was
allowed, on any pretence, to enter. Caspar
alone heeded not his black looks: he was
not his rival, so troubled nothing about them,
but talked as long as he chose to Mary, letting
Slade scowl his blackest at the broad back
which hid his sun from him.

This, I say, was the reason why Caspar
Hoffman had one enemy amongst us.

On that evening when we had the conversation as above, Caspar, with a sort of mock
gallantry, had given the girl a rose. The act
and his manner were harmless enough ; but
I felt distressed, having noticed the vivid
blush that came to her cheek as she pinned
his gift to her dress, and had now, in truth,
only led up to the subject under discussion
with a view of warning my friend not to make
the girl too fond of him.

So I resumed.

'Slade, you must know, looks upon you as
a fortunate rival. He is madly in love.'

'Then I am sorry for it. I am not his rival, although I fear he will have little chance, for all that.'

'But you really ought to be careful. I don't want to flatter you, but the girl is in love with you.'

'Then I am more sorry yet. I am *ver-sprochen*—bespoken. Far away in *Vater-land* dwells a little *mädchen*, with eyes of blue, and flaxen hair. True and tender is she; and years, weary years, has she waited for me. When I can I will send for her, or else some day I will go back to her, and till the earth, like my fathers before me, for a living.'

I said no more, and Caspar's eyes grew dreamy and far away as he fell into a deep reverie, thinking, doubtless, of the little German maiden waiting and waiting for her lover. Then he sighed, and stretching out his arm, took his clarionet, and played softly, very softly, a plaintive little phrase. It was very simple and very melodious. I was struck with it, but could not remember having heard it before. I listened attentively as he played it over and over again. A sad little tune, and one I should no doubt always have been able to recall, even if events to come had not impressed it for ever upon my memory.

When at last he laid his clarionet down, I asked him what he had been playing.

'A little *Lied*—a setting to one of Heine's songs.'

'But who wrote it? It is quite fresh to me.'

'A friend of mine, who had dreams once, such as you confess to, *mein Englander*, but who never dreams now.'

'You mean you wrote it yourself?'

He laughed and nodded, and at my request played his strange little song several times more; so that, when at last we went to bed, I rocked my brain to repose with its rhythm.

The next day, in spite of the season being summer, was bitterly cold. That evening we played on the pier, with a keen north-east wind cutting our hearts out, and making our scanty audience stamp their feet and clap their hands, more for the promotion of circulation than for applause.

I had not been well all the day. I had only done my part with a great effort; and when at length our hour of freedom came, and we shouldered our music-stands and left the pier, I think I felt worse than ever I did in my lifetime. I was thoroughly worn out, and my one desire was for warmth and rest. Hoffman and I walked together, as was our custom; and without telling him how ill I felt, I said, as we turned out of the Esplanade:

'I am shivering with cold. I think I shall step into Mrs. Deane's and get a glass of brandy.'

'Very well; although, after your lecture

last night, you cannot expect me to accompany you. I shall go home and write a letter.'

I entered the inn, and found the dark-browed Slade there as usual. The spirits I drank seemed to do me little or no good : but as the gas was lit, I found the warmth of the room pleasant ; so I sat down in a corner, and, thoroughly ill and tired out, dozed off. I must have slept a long time, for the sound of the shutters being put up for the night aroused me. I opened my eyes, and from the dusk of my corner saw Stephen Slade leaning over the counter, talking to Mary Deane, who kept well out of his reach.

'I tell you I love you,' I heard him whisper. 'I will slave day and night until I can make a home for you, if you will give me one word of hope.'

'Why can't you take your answer, Mr. Slade ?' replied the girl. 'When you asked me before, I told you I cared nothing for you, and never should. Why can't you leave me alone and go elsewhere ?'

I saw the man's back shaking with suppressed passion as he said :

'If that long-legged cur of a German chose
to speak to you as I am speaking, you'd
give him a very different sort of answer, I'll
be bound.'

The girl's face flushed. 'What do you
mean by insulting me and a better man than
yourself?' she cried, with spirit. 'His friend
is sitting just behind you, so you had better
be careful what you say.'

Slade, who had doubtless forgotten my presence, faced round and looked at me. I had
the sense to shut my eyes again.

'Damn them both for upstarts,' he growled.
'The boy is drunk or fast asleep.' Then, turning again, he said in a hissing whisper, 'You
mind me, Mary Deane—I'll have you, or no
one shall. If I see that fellow making love
to you again, I'll shoot him like a dog that
he is. I will; I swear it! If it costs me
my life I will.'

The girl laughed scornfully, and without
another word turned her back upon him and
vanished through the curtained door.

After waiting a minute on the chance of
her reappearing, Slade, with a scowl and a
curse at my sleeping form, left the ·house,

whence, after a proper interval, I followed him and crawled home.

The next morning I should have told Caspar Hoffman all I had overheard, but when I awoke I found myself scarcely able to articulate a word, and suffering from severe pain in my chest. I was seriously ill—there was no doubt about it—and, moreover, rapidly growing worse. That evening I was taken to the hospital, where I lay for a fortnight, with inflammation of the lungs. Caspar, like a good fellow, came to see me every morning and evening, until within a day or two before I was pronounced well enough to quit. When that time came and I stepped outside the gates, I felt it would be some time before I could resume my place in the Upper Rhine Band. Slowly, very slowly, I walked home, wondering what had kept Hoffman away from me for the last few days, and looking forward to the cheery greeting he would give me when we met. Just before I reached our house I encountered Stephen Slade. To my surprise he stopped, and accosting me with quite a show of friendship, inquired after my health, congratulated me upon my recovery, and even carried his new-born civility far enough to beg me to take some dinner with him, it being now the time allotted for that meal. I began to think that it might be, after all, I had mis-judged the man—that his roughness was but external, and his heart beneath as kind as other people's hearts. However, as I was anxious to get home and see my friend, I declined his well-meant hospitality, saying that Hoffman would be expecting me.

'Hoffman!' he repeated. 'Have you not heard the news?'

'What news?'

'Hoffman has left us—suddenly—without a word to any one. He has gone back to Germany, we all believe. Every one thought you were in the secret.'

So saying, he bade me good morning, leaving me too much surprised to utter a word.

I entered the room in which Caspar and I had lived together for the last two months, and the first thing I saw was a letter lying on the table. It was addressed to me. I opened it; it ran thus:

'DEAR FRIEND,—

'I am called back to Germany at an

hour's notice, and deeply regret that I cannot find time to see you again. Please guard all my belongings, and I will write telling you where to send them. My prospects being entirely changed, I shall return no more.'

Ill, weary, disappointed, and sorely in need of companionship and sympathy as I was, I sank down on one of the rickety chairs, leant my head upon the table, and fairly cried.

The letter was unsigned, but its being written in that peculiar German caligraphy left no doubt as to who was the writer. After our daily and almost brotherly intercourse, Caspar's abrupt departure seemed almost unkind; yet I felt that he was such a true friend to me, that he must have had strong reasons for it, and also for withholding his present address. I could only hope that soon I might hear from him.

In another week I had recovered my health sufficiently to enable me to resume my place among my Teutonic comrades, and found, upon rejoining them, an idea prevailing that Caspar Hoffman had inherited a fortune—

hence the reason he had left so suddenly.

I was still weak, and lagged behind the
others as we left the pier that evening. Just
outside the toll-gate I met Mary Deane. I
suppose she must have hidden herself until
Slade had passed by. If I looked ill, she
looked worse. The rich colour had flown
from her cheeks, her lips looked drawn, and
dark circles were round her eyes. Glancing
hastily around, she said, in a sharp, quick
whisper :

' I want to see you—I must speak to you
—alone. Be outside our house at twelve
o'clock to-night without fail.' Then, without
waiting for any answer, she turned and hurried away.

Her manner was so emphatic, so earnest,
that I never thought of disobeying her command, and twelve o'clock found me waiting
outside the corner house. The door opened
stealthily, and Mary, appearing, beckoned me
in. I entered, then, taking my hand, she
led me to the parlour. The gas, turned down
low, made a dreary twilight in the room, and
through it the girl's face looked wan and

ghost-like. I seated myself, wondering what
was the reason of this midnight appointment,
when, leaning over me, she whispered in my
ear :

'Where is Caspar Hoffman ?'

'Caspar Hoffman!' I repeated. 'Why,
gone home to his friends and to fortune, they
say. He left me a letter—read it.' And as
I spoke I drew the letter from my pocket.

She waved it aside without giving it one
look. 'He has not,' she said; 'he is dead—
murdered—and that man has murdered him.'

'You are dreaming, or you must be mad.'

'I am not. I know it. I am sure of it.
He threatened to do so the night you were
taken ill, and he has done it now. When or
how I know not; but every time I see his
black face and wicked eyes I can read the
deed there. Oh, my Caspar! my bonnie
Caspar! I will find out the truth.'

'But his letter to me—it is written as a
German writes. Look at it.'

She turned upon me with something like
contempt in her voice.

'And would not a man who murders forge
also? Has he never seen a letter written by

a German ?   Ah, Stephen Slade is a cleverer
man than either you or Caspar ever suspected.   Do you know Caspar's handwriting ?'

I was obliged to confess I could not remember having seen it.

'Then I say that letter is only a forgery,
written to deceive us.   He has killed him.
I know it.   He comes to me in dreams, in
more than dreams, and tells me so.   You,
who call yourself his friend, aid me in bringing
his murderer to justice.   Oh, my Caspar ! my
Caspar !' and she threw her arms across the
table, and leaning her head upon them, sobbed
convulsively.

The girl's passionate words, excited manner,
and, above all, absolute, unswerving belief in
her wild statement, greatly impressed me.
Her dark suspicions were infectious ; and as
my former opinion of Slade again reasserted
itself, I began almost to think that her horrible fancy might have some foundation.   It
may have been my ill-health, or the mystery
of this midnight meeting, that induced me to
give any weight to her words ; but, any way,
I promised to leave no stone unturned, but

try and ascertain whether Hoffman had really
written the letter, and whether he had gone
back to Germany or not. Calmed, apparently,
by my promise, she bade me good night.

As she opened the door for me to go out—
as her hand lay in mine—as I was looking
into her great dark eyes, shining through the
dusk—solemn at one moment with the horror
they pictured ; fierce at another with fire of
revenge—as we stood thus, I say, a sound
came on the night wind—a sound that sent a
tremor through me and made the blood in
every vein run cold with unspeakable fear.
And I knew, from the way in which her
fingers closed on mine, that as I heard it and
trembled, so it was with my companion.   It
was nearly one o'clock.   The street was deserted by all save ourselves.   So quiet was
all around, that we could catch the dash of
the waves on the shingle, audible, even at
that distance, through the stillness of the
summer night ; and then—soft, yet clear and
well defined—rose, as it were close to us, a
strain of plaintive music.   So close it seemed,
that I turned instinctively to see the player ;
but we were alone in the street, which,

although dimly lighted, held no recess where one might hide ; and I felt, soft as the music sounded, it was not distance that diminished the power of the notes. Whoever or whatever produced it, was almost within arm's-length. And bar after bar of the strange music came sighing to us, until at last I had recovered sense enough to understand the language of the notes, and then my fear was linked with horror, for this was the melody that fell upon my ear :

Over and over again I heard the pathetic

little phrase floating, it seemed, in the air around me ; at times so low that I could scarcely say I heard it—at times so clear and distinct that I turned again and again to detect the player, but each attempt was futile.

Many minutes did Mary Deane and I stand, hand in hand, listening with all our power, neither speaking nor trying to speak, until the notes grew fainter and fainter, and finally died into the silence of the night, and the distant murmur of the waves was the only sound left.   I looked into the girl's face, but said nothing.

'You heard it ?' she whispered.

I nodded assent—my agitation was too great for speech.

' I did not tell you before,' she said ; ' but I have heard it three times.   But never so clearly or for so long as to-night.   What does it mean ?   Tell me.'

' I do not know,' I replied ; and then with an effort added, ' let us meet here again to-morrow night at the same hour, and try and find out its meaning.'

She assented, and closed the door as I

turned away towards my home. Agitation is no word to express the state of my mind; for, although I dared not tell Mary Deane so, the unearthly melody that came sighing so softly to us that night was that same plaintive little air that Caspar Hoffman had played to me the last time we had sat together in the room which now, without his cheery presence, seemed so desolate.

I knew not what to think—what to do. My sleep that night was restless, broken, and dreamful. All sorts of horrors came to me, but running through and in some way entwined with every dream was that haunting melody. The figures in my visions moved to its notes; their voices, when they spoke, kept time to them. I seemed to breathe to their rhythm; and glad I was when I awoke altogether and found it was broad daylight.

Somehow I dragged through the next day, studiously avoiding Stephen Slade's eyes, lest he should read in my look the growing but as yet undefined suspicions I felt my eyes must utter. At half-past nine I threw myself on my bed and slept with my clothes on for three hours. At one o'clock I was waiting

outside the inn.   There was no moon, but
the stars were bright above.   I had not long
to wait ; the girl soon appeared, and closed
the door behind her.   Her head was covered
with a thick hood which almost prevented
recognition.

We shook hands, and, without a word,
waited with nerves intent on catching the
first strains of the mysterious music, if indeed
it should be again audible to us.   For some
time we listened in vain, and I was just on
the point of saying, ' It must have been our
fancy,' when close at my right hand arose the
plaintive and familiar strain.   Mary's cold
fingers stole trembling into mine as, in spite
of last night's experience, I turned sharply
round, feeling convinced that some bodily
player must be close by.

Up and down the street I looked, but we
were alone, and yet the notes lay on the air.
Now they seemed at the right, now at the
left, now behind, now in front—departing,
returning, circling around, yet ever with us.
I am not ashamed to say dread—mortal
dread—came over me, as with a mournful
monotony I heard, over and over again,

Caspar Hoffman's sad little melody sighing through the night, whilst, with her hand ever in my own, the girl and I stood still, knowing neither what to do nor how to account for the phenomenon.   At last, in an awe-struck whisper, Mary Deane said :

'It is Caspar playing. I know it is—I feel it.   What are we to do ?'

The sound of her voice recalled my reasoning faculties, and, unbeliever as I had ever been in the supernatural, I felt now that it might be for some weighty reason we were permitted to hear this strange music on these two occasions.   I was brave now ; fear had left me.   I was only eager to learn what message the music bore.

I drew my companion's arm through mine.

'Let us move up the street a few paces, and see if the music follows us,' I said.

We did so, but after walking some twenty yards could hear it no longer.   Then we returned to the spot where at first we stood, and the notes sounded as before.   We then walked a little way in the other direction, and yet we heard the melody : farther yet we went, and it was with us ; farther and farther yet, right to the end of the street, and yet it kept near us. We turned to the left, and heard it not. We retraced our steps, and took the road to the right, and clearly we heard each note once more.

We neither were frightened now : my companion, like myself, had caught the meaning of the music. It was not accompanying us, nor following us, but, as a bird might, hovering before us—guiding us for some purpose, to some end, although we knew not to what or whither it might lead us. The girl seemed transformed. Her step grew firm and sure ; her arm trembled on mine no longer. She turned her wild eyes to mine, and said, almost in exultation :

'I knew it—I knew that music meant something. Listen ! it calls us to follow, and it will lead us on and on until we learn the truth. Yes, my Caspar, my love,' she continued, speaking in a softer voice, as if addressing one near at hand—' yes, follow it we will, even to the ends of the earth.'

She said no more ; and silently, for what seemed hours, we followed as the music led us. All fatigue had left me, and every nerve was strung with excitement and curiosity. Far along the main road we went, turning neither to the right nor the left, with the music ever circling and floating around us, but ever advancing, as the mother bird that seeks to draw the stranger from her nest and its treasure. On and on for perhaps three miles it led us by the road, till, glancing back, I could only see the lights of Shinglemouth dim in the distance. Then the notes stayed, and near us was a gate. We passed through it, and the music passed before us. We entered a grove of pine-trees, with which the country round about is thickly studded. Spectral and weird the trunks looked as they threw their straight shadows on the light brown ground beneath, carpeted many inches deep with cast needles. The pungent aromatic odour of the pines perfumed the air, and to this day that odour sets my heart beating with the memories it evokes. Then out again to the open, with nothing between us and the clear stars shining overhead.

We were now on the sward that stretched away towards the sea-cliff. There was no

road, not even a footpath over the springy
turf ; but on and on our feet were led, straight
as the crow flies—the girl's step ever falling
in unison with mine, and as firm and resolute.
Gradually we seemed to be bearing across
the downs towards the sea ; and I was
wondering whether our destination was the
sea-coast, when I found we were descending
the side of a deepish hollow. We reached
the bottom, which was thickly covered with
large-sized stones, and then with one accord
we stopped short, for we heard the music no
longer. Suddenly as it came, so it went ;
one moment we heard it, as we had heard it
for so long, close at hand ; the next, and not
a sound broke the stillness of the night. I
raised my eyes and peered around. Just in
front of us was a small, square, grey building ; old and venerable it looked, like a ruin
of some sort. The sides of the hollow in
which we stood sloped upwards towards its
roof, which seemed almost on a level with
the higher ground. As I knew but little of
the neighbourhood round about, I turned to
the girl.

‘ Where are we ?’ I asked.

' At the old lime-kiln, about five miles from home.'

' Is it worked now ?'

' No; it hasn't been worked for years. No one ever comes near it.'

'What shall we do now ?'

' I shall wait,' she answered decisively.

' Wait !' I echoed ; 'for what ? The music has left us. It has led us here, but perhaps can do no more. Its mission is accomplished. Let us return by daylight and try if we can find out anything.'

' No matter—I shall wait. You can leave me if you like ; I am not afraid.'

This was entirely out of the question ; so, finding persuasion useless, I determined to make the best of it. After all, some inner voice which I could not hear might be telling the girl what course to take. I pressed her no more, but begged her to sit down and rest herself, and upon her complying, seated myself beside her and longed for the morning to break.

And thus we sat and waited — neither speaking—both listening for the weird music to come again for our guidance—sat until I feared we should be numbed with cold, for we were not far from the sea, and the night was chilly.

Being summer-time, the nights were very short, and with joy I saw at last the welcome greyness tempering the eastern sky. With the coming dawn a mist seemed to be gathering, and a cold wind began to blow in from the sea. I was shivering, and suggested to my companion, who sat motionless as a statue beside me, that it would be well if we took shelter under the side of the lime-kiln. She made no remark, but rising, followed whither I led her. I placed her as comfortably as I could; and then, pressing her hands on her eyes, she sat silent, ever thinking, I well knew, of the man she loved.

The morning was now fairly breaking; and I was resolved, as soon as there was sufficient light, to thoroughly examine the place, and ascertain if what I dreaded to think of might be hidden there. I had even risen to begin my investigations—quietly, without disturbing my silent companion, thinking that whatever fearful discovery was to be made had better be made by me alone

—when the noise of a stone rolling down the declivity and falling with a slight crash upon its fellows at the bottom drove all the blood back to my heart. Grasping Mary's arm, I forcibly pushed her back into the darkness cast by the side of the lime-kiln, as through the grey mist of the morning a man strode down into the hollow and stood within a few paces of us; and as he stood there, for a moment we heard once more the melancholy notes that had led us so far.

The girl clutched my arm with an energy almost painful.

'See,' she whispered — 'see, there is Caspar's murderer, led here, as we were led, for us to know and accuse.'

And the man standing there with pallid face and distorted features, with great drops of sweat rolling from his forehead, was Stephen Slade. Had he looked our way he must have seen us, so close we were to each other; but all his attention seemed to be riveted on one spot, the entrance to the disused kiln, now almost hidden by a pile of stones. He was breathing hard and quick, and stood gesticulating, shaking his fists and glaring in that one direction.

'Devil! devil!' we heard him mutter, 'why will you not rest in peace and leave me alone? Three times has that cursed music drawn me here against my will. I hate you dead worse than living.'

Then, as if with an effort, he turned away and began to retrace his steps. As he moved, the girl broke from my hold and sprang after him. Her hood had fallen back, her long dark hair streamed loose about her shoulders, and her eyes from under her black and knitted brows gleamed like fire—an avenging fury she looked, claiming blood for blood. Heedless of the consequences, she grasped his arm and cried with a shrill voice, 'Murder! murder!' I had followed her, both to protect and assist her: but as I did so, the danger of bearding this desperate man flashed through my brain like lightning. As he felt her touch, I think he screamed with horror, and with a livid face staggered back, seeming about to fall. So helpless he appeared, that I believe had we then and there thrown ourselves upon him we might have bound him as easily as a child. We let the opportunity slip, and the delay was fatal. In a few moments he had recognised us ; then, knowing he had to deal with mortals like himself, not with avenging spirits, the man's horrible courage and ferocity came to his aid. His cruel eyes met mine in the early twilight ; and well, from their expression, I knew what was coming, and framed an inward prayer for deliverance.

'So you have spied and tracked me,' he said. 'You two, at any rate, will never tell the tale. I can make room for both of you beside your friend.'

Then, with fell murder written on his face, he came towards me, and I braced myself for the struggle—the struggle which I felt was hopeless.

Slade, as I said before, was a broad-shouldered man of great strength. What chance could I have with him, broken as I was with sickness, and worn out with the night-watching ? I had no weapon, not even a pocket-knife. Fly, and leave the girl to his mercies, I could not. Truly, death seemed very near to me at the moment when

I felt those muscular arms thrown round me, and my ribs bending beneath their strong grip.   I was an infant in his hands.   Yet I was not altogether unaided.   Bravely the girl stood by me, tore at his arms, at his face, to make him release me.   It was but for a moment, however.   He loosened his left arm, and, with one backward sweep of it, hurled her, stunned and senseless, upon a heap of stones.   'You and I will have another kind of reckoning by-and-by, my pretty maid,' I heard him mutter as he closed with me once more.   Death was very, very near me now.   Backwards and forwards we swayed, then we fell together—Slade uppermost.   I was utterly exhausted, and could struggle no more.   The ruffian tore himself from my feeble grip, and kneeling on my arms, pressed his thumbs upon my throat. As I lay helpless, I could look straight into his wicked eyes, but saw no gleam of mercy or relenting there.   In three seconds my head felt bursting, sense was failing me ; I seemed to be trying to articulate these words, 'How hor—ri—ble—to—die—like this !' when—waking, dreaming, or dying—I heard close, close to me, the wail of Caspar Hoffman's *Lied*—the same ghostly music that had led us to this spot, and brought the murderer face to face with us. And as I heard it, I knew I was saved. Slade's villainous grip on my throat relaxed ; I breathed once more ; and although too far gone to move hand or foot to save my life, I could see the ruffian rise, stare around him in a bewildered manner, then, muttering like one in a dream, and with a face as set as a somnambulist's, ascend the side of the hollow, and vanish over the level ground. Then I fainted.

When my senses returned I found Mary Deane kneeling beside me and chafing my hands. She had not been much injured, and upon coming to herself found me lying dead, as she thought, and Slade gone.

We were too much exhausted, indeed, too much terrified, to make any investigation that might solve the mystery of the night. Painfully we dragged ourselves over the downs until we reached the main road ; then, having removed, so far as we could, all traces of the recent deadly struggle, managed

by the aid of a passing waggon to reach
Shinglemouth before its inhabitants were
astir.

What could I do now ?   My only course
seemed to be that of going to the police and
accusing Slade of the murder of Hoffman.
I could give no common-sense reasons for
the accusation, but I might beg that the
lime-kiln be searched, and the man kept in
sight at least during the operation.   It should
be no fault of mine if Slade escaped justice.
And so I went.

The inspector whom I saw was rather a
friend of mine, and gave me an attentive
hearing.   Upon learning the gist of my
errand, he said :

'You are an hour too late.   The man is
in custody now, upon his own confession.
Says he murdered him and stuck the body in
the entrance of the lime-kiln, making a heap
of stones in front of it.   We thought him
drunk or raving--kept on talking about
music that was driving him mad.   Any way,
he's here safe enough, and some of our men
have gone off down coast to find out whether
his tale is true or false.'

And true enough they found it. Three hours afterwards I saw all that remained of my light-hearted German friend; and two months afterwards Stephen Slade was hanged at Dorchester gaol.

He simply confessed to the murder, but would enter into no particulars. Plenty of circumstantial evidence was forthcoming to establish his guilt, but it was never ascertained how he decoyed his victim to that lonely and distant spot. A pistol-bullet through the breast told the way in which the deed was done, and that was all.

Slade died sullen and impenitent. The prison doctor thought there were grounds for a reprieve, as the man was for ever talking wildly about music he, but no one else, could hear. This was, however, attributed to the profession he had followed, not to higher causes; so, as he had no friends to take up his case, and as his character was not such as to enlist strangers in his favour, no steps were taken to mitigate his sentence, and he met the fate he fully merited.

Since that night I have never heard that ghostly music. Its mission was no doubt accomplished when the mysterious power it wielded caused the murderer's hand to drop nerveless from my throat, and drove him, cruel, remorseless and impenitent as he was, to make confession of a crime that might else have remained undiscovered, and to reveal the tragic end of Caspar Hoffman.

THE BLATCHFORD BEQUEST.

CHAPTER I.

THE waves were tumbling in heavily on Oversea beach. It was too dark to see the white line of surf from the row of houses which fronted the sea, but the sullen roar of each wave as it broke, and the sharp crash of the shingle as it followed the retreating flood, were audible at a much greater distance off than Marine Parade. The wind blew in fierce gusts, sending the rain against the window-panes like a whip with a thousand lashes falling at the same moment. No one, except, perhaps, a passionate poet with a raging heart, and a constitution good enough to defy cold and wet, would, of his own free-will, be out of doors on such a night as this.

The Rev. Cuthbert Wrey, curate in charge of St. Nicholas, that little galvanized iron offshoot of St. Mary's, Oversea, was not a poet; therefore, he felt heartily glad when he arrived at the door of his lodgings in Marine Parade, without having been flattened by the force of the gale against the low walls and railings which enclose those wind-swept little gardens facing the sea. He was afraid to unbutton his mackintosh to get at his latch-key—let the wind have one fair chance, and he expected to find the garment stripped from his shoulders and blown into ribbons— so he knocked, rather impatiently, at the door.

'An awful night, Mrs. Roberts!' he said to his landlady, when, by dint of united efforts, they had closed the door and barred out the uproarious wind.

'Yes, sir; an awful night,' replied Mrs. Roberts, taking the dripping mackintosh and broad-brimmed hat. 'So awful, sir,' she added apologetically, 'that I thought it better to read a sermon at home, instead of coming to hear you this evening.'

'Quite right. Did you more good, I dare

say,' answered the curate pleasantly, and as one whose belief in the efficacy of sermons was not unassailable. 'I'm sure I wouldn't have gone to church to-night, if I could have helped it.'

Mrs. Roberts looked grave at hearing such sentiments proceed from the cloth.

'Your tea is quite ready, sir,' she said. 'Would you please take off your wet boots before you go up? They mark the stair-covering so, and washing is so expensive.'

The Rev. Cuthbert complied. He went up-stairs in his stockings; and having changed sundry dripping articles of attire, drew his chair to the table and commenced his tea or supper, or whatever the meal might be called.

Curates are not a well-paid race, and the stipend allotted to the curate of St. Nicholas, in return for the assistance he gave the rector of that dreary little watering-place, Oversea, was hardly enough to provide delicate fare, such as induces people to linger over their tables. He ate his cold meat with a healthy appetite, drained out the last drop from the teapot, filled his pipe, and rang for the tea-things to be cleared.

'You may leave the kettle, Mrs. Roberts,' he said. 'I think, after my wetting, I may indulge in a glass of hot whisky and water.'

'Quite right, sir,' said the landlady. 'Ah, it's on a night like this one pities the teeto-talers.'

'All extreme people must be pitied, Mrs. Roberts,' said the curate, smiling. 'But bring another glass with mine, and I will give you some.'

Although the good lady murmured something about only taking spirits twice a year, a second glass made its appearance, and she left the room with the materials for a comfortable nightcap in her hand.

Cuthbert Wrey pushed back the table, wheeled his chair in front of the fire, put his feet on the fender, and clasping his hands behind his head, sat watching the smoke curling from his pipe. He felt that if any man had a right to enjoy perfect rest that evening, it was the curate of St. Nicholas. He had conducted two services, and attended the afternoon classes. He had visited his sick, and, so far as he knew, done all that duty demanded of him. Now let him take his ease for an hour or two. He saw nothing to interfere with it, unless the wind should blow the windows in.

Cuthbert Wrey was a man of about twenty-eight, tall, muscular, and good-looking. His features, although strongly marked, were not irregular; indeed, a very little more would have made him a remarkably handsome man. Perhaps he looked at the worst, as we see him now with his face in repose. Its expression was not quite a happy one. It bore at times a kind of dissatisfied look— a look which, it seemed, might soon grow habitual. His brows had a trick of frowning until they almost met, and at the same time the corners of his mouth fell in a slightly scornful manner—whether in scorn at the world in general, or himself in particular, it is doubtful if he could have determined. Anyway, his face was not exactly the face of a happy, successful, or contented man. Yet, when he spoke—even when another's affairs occupied his mind, and he was not thinking

of Cuthbert Wrey—this expression completely vanished. His words were kind, and
the smile which accompanied them always
frank and pleasing as the words themselves.
Altogether, he was a great favourite with both
the rich and poor of Oversea.

He did not look very clerical as he sat in
the shabby armchair. His long black coat
had been replaced by a comfortable loose fitting garment, a relic of his Oxford days ; sad
enough in its decay, but not in its hue.

Well-earned as his rest was, he did not seem
to enjoy it much. He gazed on his smoke-
clouds for a long time, and the dissatisfied
expression on his face deepened. Then he
sighed, and releasing his right hand, swept it
round with a kind of hopeless gesture. His
arm was a long one, and, in the circuit it
made, came in contact with the black sermon-
case which he had deposited on the mantel-
piece, and which contained the discourse he
had so recently delivered to the scanty congregation who had braved the weather. It
fell at his feet ; and with a grim smile on his
face, Cuthbert let it lie.

'It is no use,' he said, looking at the ill-

treated sermon, and apparently addressing his
remarks to it—' it's no use. How can I expect to convince others, if I can't convince
myself? I wrote that sermon for myself; I
preached it for myself, not for my flock ; yet
I am more full of doubt than before. The
hard work, the penury, I did not mind, until
I began to doubt. There must be an end to
this. Why did I take orders ?' he continued,
looking fiercely at the passive sermon-case.
' Why did I take orders ? Now, to answer
that question, a man must know himself better
than I do. I had to make my living in one
profession or another. I was ambitious, and,
I believed, clever. The Church was easy to
enter, and I may have fancied there was a
career there for a clever man. It was no
wrong to think this ; for in those days I believed I could do my duty as a clergyman.
Then my frame of mind at the time !'—here
his eyes grew sad and his voice dropped.
' Margaret had just died. She never knew I
loved her; but I knew it. And then, Travers—ah, Travers, Travers, my friend! with
your sweet childlike trust in every old tradi-
tion—your silvery tongue—you are answer-

able for my mistake. Those walks together, those arguments of yours, the fervid eloquence of which so moved me, that for a time I could see all things by your own light! And you, I hear, were last month received into the bosom of Rome. You will scarcely blame me. Certainly, in leaving the Church, I shall not be accused of self-interested motives. I have nothing in view. On the other hand, I don't make much sacrifice. Fifty shillings a week is not a great income for a man to earn. I will set about making the change at once.

'Well, Mrs. Roberts, what is it?' he asked testily, as his landlady knocked, entered, and cut short his meditations in a moment.

'Some one from "The Folly," sir, with this note.'

'Mrs. Blatchford is worse, I suppose,' said the curate, opening the note. It contained a few hastily written lines from the doctor: 'I am afraid Mrs. B. cannot last out the night. She is anxious to see you. Come at once.'

'Poor woman!' ejaculated Cuthbert. 'So much better she seemed yesterday, and now dying.'

'Is she, indeed, poor thing?' said Mrs.
Roberts, with a sympathetic face.

'Yes; I must go at once.' He took off
his lounging-coat, preparatory to assuming his
clerical garb. 'I don't know how I shall get
there through this weather.'

'There is a carriage waiting, sir.'

'Then go down, and say I shan't be a
minute.'

Cuthbert attired himself as quickly as he
could. Then, with a half-sigh, he took his
pocket communion-service, and prepared himself for the solemn duty before him. 'I wish,'
he said gravely, 'that this sacred rite was to
be performed by some one who does not reek
of tobacco like I do.' He felt it no grievance
to be called from his fireside. Duty was
clear enough, and no doubts harassed him
on that score. He would have gone as will-
ingly to the poorest member of his congregation, or of anyone else's congregation, who
needed his aid, as he went to the richest lady
in Oversea, as Mrs. Blatchford was reputed
to be. He spoke a pleasant word to the
coachman, who sat, a shapeless bundle of
wraps, on the box, and entered the brougham,

which drove off as fast at the horses could draw it.   It was not at a great rate of speed, for the road was steep and the gale still at its height, blowing the reins into graceful curves, beginning at the driver's hands and ending at the horses' bits; even at times threatening to overturn the carriage entirely.

The dying woman lived in a large house on the top of the hill overlooking Oversea.   In whatever part of the town you stood, you could see that house.   When first built, it had been christened some high-sounding name; but that name had long since vanished. Nicknames often cling to people and to things much longer than their proper names, and for years this house had been known as 'The Folly,' or sometimes as 'Barnes' Folly.'   The original Barnes, from whom it derived this distinction, was a sanguine man, who had imbibed the notion that, with proper treatment, Oversea was destined to become one of the most fashionable seaside resorts in England.   He was a tradesman who had made money in the place, and claimed for it natural advantages which few others could be persuaded to see.   His theory was, that if

suitable residences were erected, people of
station and importance would flock to them.
The feeling was patriotic, honourable, and
ruinous.   He tested the truth of it by building a huge house on the very top of the hill.
It cost him several thousands of pounds, and,
when finished, no one could be tempted either
to buy it, or even to rent it.   Lacking a
tenant, Mr. Barnes lived there himself for
some years—he could scarcely be said to
occupy it; being a bachelor, his belongings
and himself barely filled a corner.   By-and-
by some other speculations went awry ; Mr.
Barnes was ruined, and died eventually in the
county union.   Then the mortgagee took
possession, and finding another sanguine
man, sold him the house for about one-third
of the sum it cost Barnes.   After that it made
a few intermittent, spasmodic, and unavailing
efforts to earn a livelihood.   At various times
it was a boarding-house without boarders, an
hotel without guests, a school without pupils,
and a hydropathic establishment without
patients.   Then it gave up the battle, and
for several years lay void and lethargic—its
only use in the world being that of serving as

a capital landmark to the Channel pilots, or a warning to speculators who might fancy that Oversea could be made anything of.

Shortly after Cuthbert Wrey entered upon his duties as curate of St. Nicholas, Barnes' Folly took a new start. The gossip of the place said that a rich widow, now the owner of the deserted mansion, had made up her mind to reside in it. It is not clear how Mrs. Blatchford became possessed of such an undesirable property ; probably it was by way of mortgage ; but it had been hers for several years, and her intentions were as gossip asserted. The shuttered windows were once more opened; painters, plasterers, and paperhangers spent a busy and profitable three months in the house ; van-loads of furniture arrived, and Barnes' Folly was again inhabited.

As no one save an eccentric person would have lived from choice in such a house, the Oversea folk were not surprised at finding that Mrs. Blatchford was eccentric. She was a widow of about fifty-five—without, so far as people knew, son, daughter, or near relative. She was haughty as a Spaniard, proud as Lucifer, and cold as the east wind. She lived in dreary solitude in the big house, neither going into society nor entertaining company. That she was rich, was self-evident ; but no one knew the true extent of her wealth. To those of her own station with whom chance brought her into contact, she was repellantly polite; to her inferiors, she was rigidly just. She subscribed to the various local charities in a severe, business-like, but substantial manner ; and, although living alone, her establishment was conducted on a liberal scale most comforting to the Over-sea tradesmen. She drove about in her great carriage, a stately solitary lady; and with the exception of Cuthbert Wrey, no one in the neighbourhood could be said to stand on terms of friendship with her.

Curiously enough, between Mrs. Blatch-ford and the curate something very much like friendship had for some years existed. As in duty bound, he had called upon her shortly after her arrival. It may be, his natural manner and pleasant words made an impression upon her—anyway, he had not found her so stern and repellant as she appeared to her other visitors. A little while afterwards, he had been able to render her a trifling service, or so it appeared ; but which had in all probability saved her house from becoming the prey of burglars. Since then, the solitary lady had shown him decided marks of her favour. Cuthbert was a gentleman, and if a very poor one, perfectly independent—far too much so to let the rich lady imagine she was in any way condescending by showing him friendship. Moreover, he was a clever, clear-headed man, such as a woman likes to consult when any difficulties arise in her business affairs. So Mrs. Blatchford found not only his society entertaining, but, on occasions, his help and advice valuable. Thus it was that he was the one person she seemed glad to see ; and for a long time he had been, if not the only visitor, the only welcome visitor at The Folly.

On his side, when he had penetrated the veil of reserve with which she covered herself, Cuthbert found her an intellectual, well-informed woman. From chance remarks, he decided that her nature had been spoiled and her life soured by some great grief ; and he

soon found that she possessed an iron will,
and determination to have her own way at
any cost. Yet she was not exacting or un-
reasonable; and to him, whose interests could
in nowise clash with her own, she appeared a
sincere, if somewhat undemonstrative, friend.
It can scarcely be said that he loved her—
her nature was not a lovable one—perhaps it
was good-natured pity for her loneliness that
induced him to visit her so often, and to
trouble himself about her affairs. Certainly
it was with no thought of personal advantage,
unless it were for the use of her well-stocked
library; although malicious people—chiefly
Dissenters, who knew not Cuthbert—wagged
ill-natured tongues, and prophesied that one
day the strangely assorted pair of friends
would forget the disparity of their years.

During the last few months it had been
the man's turn to want an adviser. His
doubts as to his fitness for the profession he
had chosen needed to be ventilated. Each
day, the feeling that he must no longer
remain in the Church grew stronger and
stronger; yet he dreaded taking the final
step. Mrs. Blatchford had given him good

counsel, and advised him to act as honesty
of purpose impelled him.   Only the day before she was taken ill, she had said, with
more feeling than he had ever known her
exhibit :

'Mr. Wrey, you are my friend—perhaps
my only friend.   I can see you are troubled.
Make an end of this, and be yourself once
more.   I am as fond of you as I am of any
one in the world.   I am old enough to be
your mother.   If you want money for a fresh
start in life, you must take it from me.'

Cuthbert had declined the offer, firmly but
gratefully. If he left the Church for conscience'
sake, he must make some sacrifice, or he would
not feel right in his own mind.   Still, he was
glad to think that this stern, proud woman
was so kindly disposed towards him.

Since that day, he had not seen her.   The
next day she was taken seriously ill, and
doctors and nurses were summoned.   Of
course he had called regularly until to-day,
when his duties had been so heavy he could
not find time to mount the hill.   And yesterday he had heard she was so much better.

The horses struggled bravely to the top of

the hill on which The Folly stood, braving the fury of the storm. A grave servant, whose face spoke of impending calamity, showed Cuthbert into the library, where the doctor joined him.

'She has been delirious all day,' he said, 'calling for her son.'

'Her son! Has she a son?' asked Cuthbert, surprised.

'She must have; and by the way she talks, I should think he had been but little joy to her. Consciousness returned about an hour ago, but it means the end. She asks for you continually, and you are barely in time. Come with me.'

He was barely in time. Mrs. Blatchford was dying fast. Her aquiline features were sharp and drawn; but her face bore a softer expression than Cuthbert could remember having seen upon it. He knelt beside her and took her hand. Seeing she strove to speak, he leant his ear close to her lips.

'Under my pillow,' were the only words he could catch.

He put his hand as directed, and drew forth a letter addressed to himself.

'Shall I read it?' he asked softly.

The slight movement she was able to make was a negative one. Cuthbert again bent down to catch her faint words.

'Read it,' she gasped—'after my funeral— alone. Promise—swear you will obey it to the letter.'

'So far as I consistently can, I swear—I promise, on my honour as a gentleman.'

His words seemed to satisfy her. He felt the faintest pressure of her fingers; then, like one who has done with worldly things, she sank once more into stupor. The doctor, until now, had, from feelings of delicacy, drawn aside. He came near and shook his head ominously. Nothing more could be done.

Yet she awoke again. Her fingers tightened round Cuthbert's, and her disengaged hand seemed trying to find him through the darkness. She even spoke again; and her voice, although faint, was distinct and passionate.

'My son—my only child! You have come back at last—at last! But it is too late! I forgave, but I could not forget. I have done it for the best, darling.—He is a true man, and will keep his oath.—Good-bye! You have come back, and I fear nothing.'

So Honoria Blatchford died, happy in the merciful delusion that the hand she held was that of the son with whom, years ago, she had parted in anger, and whom she had never since seen.

CHAPTER II.

CUTHBERT rose, and gently disengaging his hand, left the room.   The letter he placed in his breast, wondering even in his grief what the contents could be.   He waited down-stairs until the doctor joined him.

'We can do nothing else,' that gentleman said. 'Let us go home.'

The carriage was in readiness, and took them to their respective abodes.

'Poor woman!' said the doctor, as they parted; 'what a dreary, lonely death.   She seemed to have no friend except you.   If you know her lawyer's address, you had better

telegraph the first thing in the morning.
Who are her near relatives ?'

'She has none.   She told me once her
relatives were all distant ones, and she liked
none of them.   I will telegraph, as you sug-
gest.'

'You will be certain to come in for a
good thing,' continued the doctor, rather
enviously.

Cuthbert started.   He had not considered
the probability, and felt annoyed at the
remark.

'I neither believe nor expect it,' he said.
'We were friends, and that is all.'

'Well, wait and see.   Good-night, if you
won't come in,' said the doctor, as the carriage
stopped at his door.

Cuthbert went to his room, raked together
his smouldering fire, and for a long time sat
thinking over the death-bed scene.   He felt
truly sorry at the loss of a friend, and, with
all her peculiarities, a true friend ; yet, in his
sorrow, he could not help wondering what
could be the contents of that mysterious
letter lying before him.   It must have been
written when Mrs. Blatchford was in good

health, as the writing on the cover was firm
and powerful. Well he knew that plain but
characteristic handwriting—just the sort one
would have expected from a stern and strong-
minded woman. But speculation was idle;
for some days he must remain in ignorance of
the wishes he had so solemnly promised to
see carried out ; so he locked the letter in his
desk in company with the maltreated sermon,
which Mrs. Roberts had picked up and
reverentially placed on the table ; then,
feeling worn-out with the work of the day,
he went to bed and slept an untroubled
sleep.

At an early hour next morning Mr. Harding, solicitor, Lincoln's Inn Fields, learned
that one of his best clients was dead ; and by
the first possible train he made his appearance at Oversea. He looked rather curiously
at the curate as they met, and his manner was
polite, if not deferential. Cuthbert was glad
to see the legal adviser appear so promptly,
thinking his advent would shift all responsibility from his own shoulders.

'And what day will you fix for the funeral,
Mr. Wrey ?' asked the solicitor, after hearing

what little there was to hear about his client's rather sudden death.

'What day will I fix?'

'Yes. If you don't know it, I may as well tell you that unless Mrs. Blatchford has made a fresh will within the last few months—a most unlikely event, as we were entirely in her confidence — entirely — unless she has made a new will, you are the sole executor.'

'I am!'

'Yes, you; and I may add, a beneficiary to a considerable extent. Our client was a strange woman, Mr. Wrey—strange and eccentric; but perfectly sane — perfectly sane.'

'No one who knew her could doubt that.'

'No—fortunately, perhaps, for you—no. The will is in duplicate. You will find one copy in her secretaire; the other is at our office. For form's sake, you had better ask her relatives, although they are but distant ones.'

'I don't even know their names, so must leave it all to you, Mr. Harding.'

'Then I will send you a list. Saturday would suit me very well, if you wish me to

come down and pay the last tribute of respect
to my poor client—I may say friend.'

' Saturday be it, if it rests with me,' replied
Cuthbert, who was longing to be alone in
order to digest Mr. Harding's intelligence.

What did it mean ?   The lawyer's enigmatical and impressive words—the promise
given to the dying woman, and in the back-
ground the sealed letter ?   He thought about
it long, earnestly, and anxiously. He guessed
that the dead hand laid some heavy burden
upon him, and he longed to know what it
might be, feeling that no weight could be
heavier than the suspense he must endure
during the five days which must elapse before
he could open that mysterious letter.   But
again and again he vowed, as a true man, he
would carry out in their entirety the wishes of
the dead woman, though he longed for the
day to come when he might set his mind
at rest as to what was required of him.

It came at last.   He had followed Mr.
Harding's instructions, and cousins bearing
the name of Blatchford, and cousins bearing
other names, assembled in Oversea.   The
rector, as was due to his richest parishioner,

performed the ceremony, which, for the con-
venience of those who came from a distance,
was fixed as late as the light would allow.
Then the mournful party assembled in the
large dining-room at The Folly, and Mr.
Harding read the will. It was short—very
short. If any of the hearers fostered hope, it
only lived through fifty lines of clerkly writing
on a sheet of foolscap. The testatrix kept no
one long in suspense. A few generous but
not absurd legacies to old servants, a couple
of charitable bequests, and then—whilst the
most stoical of the relatives held his breath or
fidgeted in his chair—the whole of the resi-
due, real and personal, to my friend, Cuthbert Wrey, clerk in holy orders—he to be
also sole executor. That was all ; too plain,
too simple, not to be fully understood by the
most commonplace intelligence. There was
no outward evidence of disappointment, no
outcry, no passionate or scandalous scene.
No cousin had been sanguine enough to
think his chance worth much, and each one
had the consolation of knowing that if he got
nothing, his kin were in the same plight. All
had been prepared for disappointment. For

many years Mrs. Blatchford had held little
communication with her family. She had
responded, as a duty, to any appeals for
assistance made by the most needy members;
but no one had been foolish enough to expect
the reversion of any part of her wealth. So,
after all, the Rev. Cuthbert Wrey was the
most astounded of the party.

He seemed dazed. He scarcely heard the
lawyer's whispered congratulations or his old
rector's outspoken ones. He bowed mechanically as the majority of the cousins filed from
the room. The very magnitude of the bequest told him that something lay behind the
words of the will. Had he been given five,
ten, even twenty thousand pounds, he might
have recognised it as an act of generous
friendship. But all—everything! The dead
woman's last words rang in his ears; the
letter, lying in his desk at home, rose before
his eyes. Whatever that will might say,
Cuthbert knew that its true meaning lay in
that sealed cover, and his only wish was to
get home and learn his fate. He could bear
the uncertainty no longer. The only persons
left in the room were the lawyer, the rector,

and two little knots of antagonistic cousins, who had recovered from their surprise, and were conversing in low but excited tones at opposite windows.

'I feel bewildered,' he said, rising and draining a glass of wine. 'I must go home and think it over quietly.'

'Quite right, my dear boy,' said the rector, whispering as he shook hands : 'Don't trouble about to-morrow. I will take the whole service at the church, and Tinley shall come round to St. Nicholas.'

'I dare say you will run up to town and see me next week,' suggested Mr. Harding ; 'or, if you like, I will come down again.'

'Yes, yes; I will come up,' said Cuthbert.

Then he left the house, and walked home to Marine Parade.

He went to his room, shut and locked the door, then took out the letter. From force of habit, he wheeled his chair round to its usual position in front of the fire, and prepared to set his mind at rest as to the true value of the will which he had so lately heard read. He had actually torn the cover open—in another minute he would have known all—when a temptation rose, stood before him, and stared him in the face—a temptation so perfectly organized, with each feature so sharply and clearly defined, that it might have owned a palpable and tangible form. *Should he destroy the unread letter?*

Cuthbert Wrey, like every other son of Adam, had many times in his life been tempted to sin, error, or folly ; but never as yet to commit an act which would in his own eyes and in the eyes of the world rank as base dishonour. His first sentiment was that of surprise—surprise at such a thought presuming to invade his brain—so, in scorn and anger, he bade it begone and trouble him no more. But the thought remained—it remained, and every moment gathered strength, purpose, and cohesion. It spoke with thrilling words ; it woke old dreams ; it unfolded wings, and bore him to the top of a mental mountain, and bade him gaze on the future and the glories thereof ; whilst, like a strange rhythm, the words of the will beat upon his ears : ' All my real and personal estate to my dear friend, Cuthbert Wrey.' He sat motionless,

the half-opened letter in his hand, in front of
him the glowing coals, which in three seconds
could reduce the paper he held to tinder.

The thoughts, the ideas, the visions which
crossed his mind during the hours he sat there,
unable to do what was right, and unwilling to
do what was wrong, would fill a book.   He
knew enough of his friend's affairs to guess that
the wealth of which she had to dispose was
great.   It was not a question of a few paltry
hundreds which tempted him ; nor, to do him
justice, was it the possession of great riches.
It was the career those riches would open to
him ; for, although not a brilliant success in
the calling he had chosen, Cuthbert Wrey
had not lost faith in himself or his talents.   It
was not common greed that assailed him,
although the stake, he knew, was a large one.
He saw himself freed from a profession for
which he had no love ; he saw wealth open
the doors of public life to him, and the dream
of younger days realized.   He even saw himself famous and wielding power.   Yes ; from
the pinnacle which commanded the future,
the winged thought showed him all this, and
more ; urging him, for the sake of these things,

to laugh at scruples, and to turn his back on
what men call honour. And hour after hour
he sat with beads of perspiration on his brow,
the letter trembling in his trembling hands ;
whilst below him, and so near, the fire threw
out little spits and darts of flame, as though
urging him to commit the secret to its keeping, and let it be hidden for ever and ever in
the depths of its wicked red heart.

He yielded again and again in theory ; but
he could not bring himself to do so in deed.
However the conflict might end, there was
one thing he felt he would not do—he would
not read that letter before he destroyed it.
Its message should perish with it. If he
committed crime, he would remain in ignorance as to its extent and influence on other
people's destinies. Only if right and honour
conquered, would he read. So he sat on
and on, making a good fight—sat until the
fire died out. He would not trust himself to
replenish it, and almost laughed as a fantastic
thought came to him—how sullen and disappointed the half-burned cinders looked.

But the candles were living, and would do
the work equally well. With a great effort

of will, he rose and extinguished them. For some time he sat in darkness ; then he found himself searching for his matches. Too well he knew why he wanted them. He struck one with an unsteady hand. It went out, but not before he caught sight of his white changed face reflected by the mirror.

'Shall I see my face like that all my life-time,' he muttered, 'if I do this thing ?'

He threw the match-box from him.

Yet the letter was still in his hand. It was as easy to tear it to pieces as to burn it. Although still mistrusting himself, he was growing stronger every minute. He groped his way to the secretaire, placed the letter in its former resting-place, turned the lock, and went to bed.

In the morning he was himself again, but feeling—if the mind may be compared to the body—as he had sometimes felt after a hard bout of football at Rugby—although rested and refreshed, with a sense of fatigue and recollection of a severe struggle still linger-ing.

' I will never laugh again at old Luther's battle with the devil,' he said, almost humbly.

' I see how easily an imaginative and superstitious man may believe in his personality.'

Cuthbert Wrey never forgot that night;
ever afterwards he was lenient, perhaps too
lenient, with transgressors; but before he
condemned, he thought of that glowing fire
and the unread letter trembling in his hand.

After breakfast he took the letter, and in a
calm business-like way sat down to read it.
It was something like he had anticipated.   It
was dated some months back, carefully worded
and written :

' MY DEAR MR. WREY,

    ' To-day I have made my will.   If I
judge you rightly, no one will be more surprised than you at its contents.   I leave you
all ; but I leave it in trust.   Years ago, my
son, my only child, left me—or I should
rather say I cast him off.   The life he had
led amply justified this step.   But he is my
son yet.   I love him ; but I dare not leave
him money to work evil with.   Where he is,
I know not, having neither seen nor heard of
him since we parted in anger.   He may be
changed, or he may change.   If so—if you

are satisfied that he is living even the life of
an ordinary man, the income arising from my
property must be his.   If he marries, or is
married, all must be settled on his children—
all except five thousand pounds, which I beg
you to accept as a token of friendship.
Should my son be dead before me, and
leave no children, take my wealth and use it
as your own, and may it bring you greater
happiness than it has brought me.   I trust
you in this as few women of my age have
ever trusted a man.   If I urged you to keep
faith, I should show doubt, and this letter
would be waste-paper.   You will read this
after my death, and will, I am pleased to
think, regret a little your friend,

                    ' HONORIA BLATCHFORD.

' *P.S.*—His name is Ralph.'

It was as he had imagined—coupling her
last words with the delivery of that letter
—she gave with one hand and took away
with the other.   Knowing Mrs. Blatchford's
character so well, he could read plainly
between the lines of that letter.   He could
see the pride which had kept her to the text,

but not to the spirit of a determination which
she had vowed should be irrevocable. However much her son had wronged her, she
had forgiven him in her heart; but having
sworn she would not leave him a penny, had
in this extraordinary way compounded with
her self-respect.

Although the passing dream of great wealth
must come no more, Cuthbert could only feel
thankful. He could with a clear conscience
accept the five thousand pounds, the interest
on which would give him about double the
income he now enjoyed. He could free himself from his bondage, and make a fresh start
under easy circumstances. So he felt very
grateful, and vowed that the instructions that
letter contained should be followed to the
best of his ability. That Ralph Blatchford
was dead, never entered his mind. He would
hear of his mother's death, and make his appearance—next week, next month or next
year, according to the distance at which his
tent was pitched. Whether he would be fit to
be trusted with the money or not, must be an
after-consideration. The decision would be
a great responsibility; but he hoped, after

last night's struggle, to be able to judge fairly. For himself, he was now a free man, with five thousand pounds; and Cuthbert went that evening to the little galvanized iron apology for a church, and preached his last sermon with a thankful heart.

After such a turn of fortune's wheel, no one wondered at his leaving his profession immediately. Legal matters were settled; the will duly proved, and although caveats were threatened by sundry relatives, the threats came to nothing; and Cuthbert Wrey, to all appearance, stepped from a curate's stipend of one hundred and twenty pounds into rents, dividends, and interest, amounting at the least to four thousand pounds a year; and as yet Ralph Blatchford had made no sign.

By Cuthbert's instructions, the notice of Mrs. Blatchford's death was inserted in the newspapers of nearly every civilized country. Then, as nothing was heard of the wanderer, the notice was changed into an advertisement requesting Ralph Blatchford to communicate with Messrs. Harding and Co., Solicitors, etc. Several impostors responded to it, and

told incredible tales, but were in turn dis-
missed. So months went on, and readers of
newspapers in all parts of the world found
the repetition of the same advertisement
growing monotonous and a trifle irritating.

Cuthbert meanwhile lived in London,
occupying inexpensive rooms, and determined to limit his expenditure to the interest
on the sum to which he was morally entitled.
He strove to keep himself from building
castles which might be shattered any moment.
He had entered for the bar, thinking that
was the best opening for his ambition. The
few people who knew him, and were acquainted with the terms of the will, wondered
at his mode of life. Why should a man of
his wealth wish to adopt a profession ? He
told no one, not even his solicitors, under
what reservation he held the property. He
worked hard, for it was his nature to do so,
and managed to live contentedly enough for
a year, willing to resign everything when
called upon so to do. Then, gradually, he
began to grow unsettled. No word or tidings
came of Ralph Blatchford. Another year
passed ; and then, only then, Cuthbert Wrey

thought—perhaps hoped—that Ralph Blatchford was known not in the land of the living.

After this, the advertisements appeared at
intervals only. Still Cuthbert feared to enter
into his kingdom.

'I will wait another year,' he said. 'Then
I shall be a barrister. If he turns up by that
time, I will try and succeed as an advocate;
if not, I must believe he is dead.'

In due time he was called to the bar; but
never held a brief nor appeared in any
court. Ralph Blatchford was still unheard
of; and Cuthbert made up his mind to use
and enter into full enjoyment of his strangely
acquired wealth.

CHAPTER III.

TEN years have passed by. It is now the
middle of August, and Parliament has some
days been prorogued. The Member for
Blacktown has gone down to his country-seat
to spend a few weeks in absolute quiet and
enjoyment of home; for although public life
sadly interferes with domestic virtues, he is a

home-loving man. He is still young; has
plenty of confidence in himself, and is content
to wait his time; trusting that when his
chance does come, he may know how to use
it. Yes, Cuthbert Wrey, the member for
Blacktown, is not only an ambitious man,
but, so far as he has gone, a successful one.

He has been in Parliament about seven
years. He could scarcely believe the truth,
when he found his first attempt successful.
No one knows exactly how candidates are
brought forward and matters managed ; but
if a man chooses to drop a hint to the proper
people that he is willing, at his own charge,
to lead a forlorn hope, it is not so very long
before he is allowed to do so.

Upon leaving the Church and taking possession of Mrs. Blatchford's wealth, Cuthbert's
one aim had been the Senate. He devoted
to this the three years' income which had
accumulated whilst he considered the inheritance in abeyance. Of course he had to wait
his chance, and that chance when offered to
him, seemed so slight that he looked upon
fighting the borough of Blacktown as advan-
ageous only because it gave him a certain

claim on his party for the future.   It was a
bye-election, and, hopeless as it seemed, was
to be contested on principle.   He went down
to try his best.   Several chances favoured
him.   The principal man in the place, his
opponent's chief supporter, turning sulky over
some trifling social piece of legislation, not
only kept Achilles-like to his tent, but gave his
dependants free license to vote as they chose.
The Government, again, had selected as a
candidate a man who was so clever that they
wanted his assistance, but who had, nevertheless, made himself so unpopular, that he
had been already rejected by two constitu-
encies.   They thought that Blacktown was a
safe seat, so sent him down there.   Perhaps
the free and independent electors resented
this, perhaps the man with great local influence did more than abstain from voting—
anyway, Cuthbert was returned by a decent
majority, and walked up to the table of the
House amid frantic Opposition cheers, as the
harbinger of the returning flood of power.
At the general election, which followed in
about two years, he was returned by an overwhelming majority.   He had made himself

known and popular, and more than that, the sulky man had now thrown his lot in with Cuthbert's party, and, like all renegades, was a bitter foe to his former faith.

We need not follow his Parliamentary career. Of course he was still in the second rank; but his name began to be heard in the mouths of men. He had kept himself before the public. His speeches were listened to, and, what is more, reported at length. He had made one or two hits, and people knew that when his party were in power he would fill one of the lesser offices. More than this he had no right to expect—at present.

Cuthbert has changed somewhat since we first saw him. Although in many ways the past years have improved him, he shows traces of hard work. His hair is sprinkled with grey, and there are lines of thought on his broad forehead; but he looks stalwart and strong enough to face any amount of toil and fatigue, whether bodily or mental. An erect, strongly built man, with a powerful but pleasing face, and possessing the knack of winning, not only the confidence and trust of one or two persons, but that of large audiences. Indeed, he is looked upon as one of the safest and best men of his party to address a large gathering of people. He speaks well and easily; his logic is simple and goes straight to the point; he possesses a commanding presence, and, moreover, argues as from honest conviction. He is now forty-one—quite young, in a political point of view; and if Cuthbert Wrey, whilst smoking his morning cigar under the shade of his favourite tree, sees in the immediate future very pleasant probabilities, who can wonder?

In spite of Mrs. Blatchford's wealth, she had possessed no residence save Barnes' Folly. Cuthbert had not made it his home; although to this day it remained his property, and unproductive as ever. He had purchased a small estate in the west of England; and that, except when Parliament was sitting, was his home. It was little more than a comfortable country-house with well-kept gardens and a small park. He had no wish to set up as a county magnate. His honours were to be won amid the bustling strife of cities; but he loved his home and those who filled it.

He sat lazily skimming yesterday's paper. Being some distance from a post town, letters only reached him once a day. As the newspaper gave no account of debates, his interest in it was but languid. The weather was so fine that he felt little inclination for work, although he knew that a pile of letters awaited him indoors. He looked the picture of placid content as he sat in the shade of the large sycamore tree. Few would have imagined that idle gentleman in a soft slouch-hat and old shooting-coat, whose thoughts seemed centred on the excellent cigar he was smoking, to be a rising legislator, who hoped, some day, to take an important part in the government of his country. When Cuthbert settled down to rest, he did so as he did everything else—thoroughly; he rested mentally and physically. A clump of arbutus hid the house from him, so there was nothing to disturb his even frame of mind. So comfortable he felt, that he resolved to postpone his correspondence until the evening—to sit and simply enjoy the sunshine and shade as long as he could.

Then, with the sound of merry laughter,

four children ran round the arbutus bushes.
They came in single file, headed by a sturdy
boy of nine, and whipped in by a toddling
female thing of three. They invaded and
clambered on Cuthbert, treating him as an
equal, with a happy ignorance of the important position he occupied in the world. In
breathless delight they informed him they had
'runned away.'

Then a tall and beautiful lady appeared,
shaking her head with mock severity at the
culprits. 'You rascals!' she said, 'coming
out and disturbing your father like this.—
Shall I send them in, Cuthbert?'

'Let them stay,' he answered pleasantly.
'We don't see too much of each other in the
course of the year. Public life and domestic
duties don't walk hand in hand.'

His wife leant over and kissed him.

'How delightful,' he continued, 'this perfect
rest and quiet! No dismal speeches to listen
to; no questions to ask the right honourable
gentleman; no bores airing grievances. The
very birds following our laudable August
custom, and lapsing into silence. Here I am
safe even from constituents, deputations, and

petitions.   I could almost wish it might last for ever.'

'Yet how you will be longing for work again before the recess is over!' said Mrs. Wrey, almost sadly.

'That, my dear, is man's perverse nature. Anyway, I enjoy myself now, if only in the perfect immunity from interruption and bother. I wish you would burn all my letters—un-opened—for the next week.'

How strangely a chance word brings up old memories! The remark he made about burning unopened letters sent his thoughts back a dozen years. Even now his face grew grave as he remembered how nearly he had yielded to the temptations of a certain night.

Just then a servant appeared and in-formed him that a 'person' wished to see him.

'A person! What sort of a person? Man or woman?'

'A man, sir.'

'You told him I was not to be seen by any one on business?'

'Yes, sir. But he said he had travelled

from Bristol expressly to see you on a private matter, and hoped you would spare him a minute.'

Cuthbert's first impulse was to send that person about his business ; but the old priestly habit of being at everyone's disposal still lingered about him ; so, disengaging himself from the children, he tossed the end of his cigar away, and walked across the lawn to the house.

The servant had used the term 'person' with propriety. The visitor seemed to merit rather more than the definition 'man ;' but no servant knowing his duties would have announced him as a gentleman. A thickset, strong, weather-beaten fellow, with the look of a sailor about him—a sailor dressed in un-conventional shore-clothes. His age might have been about the same as Cuthbert's, although exposure to wind and weather made him look some years his senior. He was waiting in the library, and, as the master of the house entered, he rose, making an uneasy sort of salutation. Cuthbert bade him reseat himself.

'Now, what can I do for you ?' he said.

The man looked uncomfortable, and waited a few moments before he spoke.

'I am speaking to C. Wrey, Esq., M.P. ?' he asked, evidently thinking the magic letters should be attached in conversation.

'Wants something, of course,' thought Cuthbert, as he owned to his name and honours.

'C. Wrey, Esq., M.P.,' continued the person. 'That's the name, sure enough. I wrote it down at once.'

'Well, go on, my man. Let me hear what you have to say.'

'It's like this, sir, you see. I came down from London to Bristol by express. They don't put third-class on express, so I had to get in with my betters.' ['Railway grievance,' thought Cuthbert.] 'Well, sir, there were two or three gentlemen there talking politics; they talked a deal about you, sir.'

Cuthbert was not overwhelmed at hearing of this tribute to his fame. His visitor went on. '"Extraordinary clever fellow," says one.—"A conceited chap," says another—begging your pardon, sir. I didn't pay much heed, as I don't know much about politics.

Never had a vote to sell. But, by-and-by,
one of 'em says : " Used to be a parson,
starving on a hundred a year."—" Very rich
now," says another. " How did he get his
money ?"—" Old woman named Blatchford
left him ten thousand a year, lucky fellow !"
says another. Then I got interested, Mr.
Wrey.'

Cuthbert also was growing interested.
An absurd thought crossed his mind, to be
dispelled as he looked more attentively at the
speaker.

'Well, go on,' he said.

'Would you mind telling me, sir,' asked
the man respectfully, ' if that Mrs. Blatchford
ever had a son named Ralph ? Blatchford
isn't a common name, you see.'

It was some years since Cuthbert had been
troubled by a claimant to the name of Blatchford, but he had not forgotten how to deal
with them.

'Now look here, my man,' he said sharply ;
' don't beat about the bush. If you are going
to assert that you are Ralph Blatchford, who
has been kept away all these years by un-

avoidable circumstances, say so at once, and I shall know how to treat you.'

The man looked at him in open-mouthed astonishment. He laughed aloud, then said :

'Lord love ye, sir! I'm not Ralph Blatchford. Bad chap as I've been in my time, I'd be sorry to have been such a one as him. But, bad as he was, Ralph Blatchford always looked what I don't, a gentleman. He's been dead and buried this fourteen years.'

Cuthbert had felt convinced of this for many years ; but he was not sorry to have clear proofs of his death.

'When did he die?' he asked. 'How did he die? I have been trying for years to ascertain his fate. What proofs have you of his death?'

The man gave a sort of chuckle.

'I don't know about proofs, sir ; but when you've seen a fellow with a ounce bullet making a hole in his lungs big enough to shove your two fingers into, I guess you don't want much more proof, or burial certificate either.'

'Very well. If you saw him die, tell me all about it.'

''Tisn't much to tell, sir. I was down at

San Francisco fourteen years ago this autumn.
—Know 'Frisco, Mr. Wrey ?'

Cuthbert shook his head.

' Ought to know 'Frisco, sir. *The* grandest
city in the world, but chock full of villainy.
Somehow, all the scum of the universe turns
up in 'Frisco. Suppose that's how I got
there,' he added, rather sadly. ' Well, sir,
one night I went into a drinking and
gambling shop, and sitting down there, I
saw Ralph Blatchford. I'd known him elsewhere, you see. Up I went to him and held
out my hand. " Why, Mr. Blatchford," I
said—for Dandy Ralph was always above
me in manner.—He scowled. " My name
ain't Blatchford," he said.—" All right," I
said. " Let your d—— name be what you
like, it don't matter to me." Then I walked
away; but I couldn't help keeping an eye
on him. He sat down with some men and
played cards. He seemed to be winning.
They were playing euchre.—Know euchre,
Mr. Wrey ?'

Cuthbert's education in this direction had
been neglected. He again shook his head.

The speaker continued, slowly and meditatively, as though endeavouring to solve a mental problem as he proceeded :

'Now, this is what puzzles me about Ralph Blatchford.   He must have been a fool—although we always thought him a smart clever chap—to go and play a stale, worn-out trick on men like that.   He must have been downright desperate, or fancied they would never expect him to insult their intelligence with such a poor affair.   Anyway, he *must* have been a fool.'

'Did he cheat?' asked Cuthbert.

'They all do, when they can,' answered the man simply.   'But he was clumsy at it. There was a flare-up!   Out came the shooting-irons.   I sat down as low as I could in my chair—always do that, sir, when you see a derringer drawn—and when I looked up in two seconds, Ralph Blatchford was a dying man.'

'What a place!' said Cuthbert, with a shudder.

'Well, it is a hasty, sudden-death sort of a place; but not so bad as you guess.   If that card hadn't been found on him, the man who shot would have been strung up, and his kicking all over, in less than ten minutes. But the card was there, sure enough, so no one could say anything.'

'What a death!' said Cuthbert, as his thoughts went back, and he heard the last words of affection and forgiveness spoken by Honoria Blatchford to the one whom she believed, in the delirium of the moment, to be her penitent son—her son, who, months before, had been shot down, a common cheat, in a gambling house—' what an end!'

But all doubts were now dispelled. He turned to his visitor.

'I am much obliged to you,' he said, 'for your information. What became of him, has always been a mystery till now. You must allow me to remunerate you for your trouble, and I dare say you will like some refreshment. I will order it to be sent to you.'

His visitor had not quite finished his tale.

'Thank you kindly, sir,' he said. 'I don't want any money; but I should like a bite and a sup.—But, Mr. Wrey, there's something else I want to say.'

'Speak on. What is it?'

'They carried him into a back-room, sir;

and I thought the poor chap would like to see a face he knew, so I went to him. He knew me well enough then. I sat with him till it was all over. Just before he died, he turns to me. " Dick," he says, gasping— " Dick, I've been a devil, and I'm dying like a dog. I've got a wife and a boy somewhere in England; find them out, and take them to my mother. She'll be good to them for my sake, although I don't deserve it." Those were Ralph Blatchford's last words, sir.'

Like one who dreams a dreadful dream, Cuthbert heard these words. After all these years, his fool's paradise had tumbled to pieces. A wife—a son! The very contingency provided for by the dead woman. He stared for some moments at the speaker without the power of utterance. He knew human nature too well to doubt that the man was telling the simple truth. A wife and son! waiting, perhaps, to claim what they could of the property which had been his so long.

The bearer of these evil tidings looked at him so inquisitively, that he nerved himself to make further inquiries; but when he spoke his voice was so changed that it seemed to the listener like the voice of another man.

'How is it ?' he asked—'how is it I only hear of this now—fourteen years after his death ?'

His informant looked uncomfortable, as if the pressing of the question would be unpleasant.

'I was bound for Australia, next day,' he said ; 'so I put the matter by until I could earn some money and get back to England. But I lost all I made as soon as I got it, for years and years. It was only last year I had a streak of luck, and followed it up. I haven't been in England two months. Besides,' he added, rather defiantly, 'Ralph Blatchford was no particular friend of mine ; I couldn't go hunting about England for a woman and a boy. I did see an advertisement once in a Sydney paper about him.'

'Why not have answered it ?'

'I was up in the Bush ; but I made shift to write a letter ; I sent it by a mate to the nearest post-town. He was never heard of again. Got killed, or lost in the Bush, I suppose.'

'Then you know nothing about his wife and child?'

'Nothing whatever, sir.   I'd almost forgotten about the whole affair.   Only, when I heard that talk about Mrs. Blatchford's money, her son's last words came back to me, and I felt conscience-struck like, and made up my mind to come and repeat them to you.   That's all I've got to say, sir.'

Cuthbert mused for a while.   How came it that the widow had never applied to the old lady for assistance?   Why had she taken no notice of the advertisements addressed to her late husband?   Either she was dead, or was in ignorance of her husband's true name and station in life; most likely the latter.

'What name did he pass under, when you saw him last?' he asked.

His visitor scratched his head.

'Ah, there you have me, sir; I've been trying to remember it all the way down.   I know I did hear it at the time.   Wilson, or Johnson, or some commonish name like that; but for the life of me, I don't know which.'

'How can I find out?'

'Only way I can think of is to get some
one in 'Frisco to go to "Daley's Bar"—it's
still running, I know—and ask if any one
remembers a man who was shot there
September 12th, fourteen years ago.   To
be sure, there must have been a good many
shot about that time, but some one may be
able to spot the right one.'

'Thank you.   I will do so.—Your name
is ?'

'Richard Dunn's my name.   Quay, Bristol,
will find me.   I'm trying to do something as
a stevedore.   I've a bit of money, and want
to stay in England, if I can.'

Cuthbert rang the bell, and told the servant
to minister to Mr. Dunn's wants ; then, bidding him good-morning, left the house by a
side-entrance, and, unseen by wife or children,
departed on a solitary walk through the neigh-
bouring lanes, in order to think the matter
over without interruption.

It was the worst intelligence he could have
received ; even worse, he thought, than that
of the existence of Ralph Blatchford.   Despite
the lapse of years, the restrictions were to
him binding as before.   Yet to be called

upon to surrender all to a woman and child who might be living in the lowest rank of life, perhaps in crime, seemed preposterous. Besides, now he would have to surrender more than wealth ; he must give up ambition, realized ambition, with it. Would he have the strength to conquer this time ? He feared not. But that question must be postponed for the present. However he acted eventually, whether true to his own idea of truth, whether he could bring himself to compound with his conscience, one thing was clear—Ralph Blatchford's widow and child must be found. Another day should not pass without steps being taken to insure this. When found, and the necessity of action stared him in the face, he would decide what to do. Having resolved this, he returned to the house.

Although he was now old enough to have learned the way to control emotion, Mrs. Wrey saw that something was amiss with him. When dinner was over and the day had closed, she sat beside him and looked into his face anxiously.

'Cuthbert dear, something is worrying you.

Is it a public or a private affair? I can at
least share the last.'

He drew her close to him. Should he tell
her? It was better not. Why should she
be made anxious by thinking of a calamity
which might never arrive? She knew something of the moral obligation which overrode
his legal title to his inheritance—that should
Ralph Blatchford appear, a great sacrifice
must be made; but all danger of that seemed
dispelled years and years ago.

'Do I seem worried?' he said pleasantly.
'If so, I am ashamed of myself, as it is only
a question of money. I may lose some
soon.'

His manner reassured her.

'Is that all?' she said. 'I feared it was
something worse than that.'

He kissed her upturned face, and could
not refrain from saying:

'If I lost everything in the world, you
would be the same to me, Marion?'

His wife took both his hands and gazed
earnestly into his eyes.

'Go back ten years, and answer that
question for me. Think how you first saw

me—how you took me from a dependent
position, and gave me love, trust, and everything worth living for. Oh, my husband,
how good you have been to me!'

Marion Wrey spoke the truth. In linking
his life with hers, Cuthbert had made no
grand alliance. She brought him neither
wealth nor influence. Ten years ago he had
met her at the house of a clerical friend, the
Rev. Mr. Mayne. She was a pale, sad, but
beautiful girl, who had awakened his interest
at once. For some time she had been acting
as governess to his friend's children. A faint
resemblance she bore to the first woman he
had ever loved appealed to Cuthbert; and
after seeing her a few times interest grew to
admiration, and admiration culminated in
love. He was not a man to linger long in
suspense. One day he went to her and asked
her to be his wife; pleading for the gift of
her love in so earnest a way, that she could
not fail to understand the depth of the passion
he felt. Yet the girl hesitated. She made
no secret of the fact that she loved him, but
begged for a couple of days' grace before she
gave him the promise he craved. Puzzled,

but hopeful, he left her, returning at the time specified for her answer.

Marion took his hand. 'I have thought and thought,' she said, 'but I cannot decide. Will you take me just as I am—just as you find me—without one question as to my past, or one allusion to it? My life has been a bitter one; and if I become your wife, let me bury and utterly blot out the past. Will you, can you do this?'

With a lover's impetuosity, he vowed that neither now nor hereafter did he care or would he wish to know anything save and except that she loved him; and as, without a shadow of evil in them, her clear eyes met his, he knew that he should never regret or wish to break the vow.

'If,' she said after a pause—'if you think I ask too much, go to Mr. Mayne; he knows my history. It is a sad one—so sad, that I should like to think you never heard it.'

But Cuthbert preferred to trust entirely, and keep his promise, like the loyal man he was. If there had been sorrow, let it be buried for ever. Marion's happiness was his future charge.

They were married almost immediately,
and from that hour every trace of sadness
vanished from Marion's face. Every day, her
husband thought, she grew more beautiful.
She was twenty-six when Cuthbert married
her; and now, ten years afterwards, she was
a fair, refined, dignified woman, fit to move
in the best society, and doing the honours of
her house to, often, distinguished visitors with
perfect grace and composure. Dearly as she
loved her husband, much as she longed for
his constant presence, she was no bar to the
success of his ambition. His aims were hers,
and she could make any sacrifice to compass
what he had at heart. No husband and wife
could have been better matched, and none
loved better.

Yet Cuthbert decided not to tell her the
purport of Mr. Dunn's visit, until something
more definite was ascertained. The next day
he went up to town, and made arrangements
with a noted inquiry agent to send some one
at once to San Francisco, in the hope of
getting some information about a man, name
unknown, who, fourteen years ago, was shot
like a dog in a gambling saloon. Then, dis-

missing, so far as he could, the whole thing
from his mind, he went back to what holiday
he could allow himself.

Chapter III.

I⊤ was several months before the agent returned from America.   He had been ordered
to spare neither time nor money, and had
kept his instructions to the letter, but with
little result as yet.   Having, after some
trouble, ascertained that the man who was
shot, as described by Mr. Dunn, passed under
the name of Winslow, he went to work to trace
him back.   It was a difficult task, but it
would have been even more so had not the
so-called Winslow, by sundry villainous acts,
left his memory green in the minds of some
with whom he had come in contact.   It will
doubtless seem as though the search was
begun at the wrong end; but, years ago, the
other way had failed.   From the time when
he quarrelled irrevocably with his mother,
Blatchford could be traced a certain distance;
then he disappeared.

At last the agent returned. By the merest chance he had found a man who had sailed from Liverpool in the same boat that carried Blatchford or Winslow. He, like others, had reasons of his own for remembering him. So this was the result of the inquiry: Blatchford sailed from Liverpool at a certain date, under the name of Winslow. After a short but discreditable career in various cities in North and South America, he had met his fate as described. Nothing was known about his wife.

Cuthbert heard the agent's report.

'We had better advertise for Mrs. Winslow,' that gentleman suggested.

Cuthbert considered.

'Not yet,' he said. 'Go down to Liverpool, and try and trace back from there. He was a saloon passenger, you say. Most likely he stayed at a good hotel. A list of the guests may show where he came from, as he appears to have been contented with one alias. Go down and see what you can do; but don't write me or come to me until you think the case hopeless, or until you have learnt all.'

The agent went his way; and Cuthbert knew that the time was drawing near when the old battle must be refought. He strove to dismiss the matter from his mind; but, do what he would, it was always with him. The sacrifice would now be so tremendous. Even if all went well with his party, and he had office, what good could be expected of a statesman who has only the emoluments of his place to depend upon? He must de-generate—must sooner or later become a place-seeker, when office was a matter of life and death to those he loved best in the world. No; if he gave up—as he was by his own code of honour bound to give up— Mrs. Blatchford's wealth, farewell to public life. All that would be over.

And with these thoughts always with him, dreading that each post would bring him news of the missing people, despite himself, the man's manner changed. He grew moody, pre-occupied, and silent; even the smile with which he greeted his wife and children was different—so different, that for the first time since she had been married, Marion Wrey felt unhappy and full of strange fears.

It was about a month after her husband's
last interview with the confidential agent
that Marion sat alone. Cuthbert had gone
to the north of England to speak at an important meeting, held that night in a large
town, one of the strongholds of his anta-
gonists. Although—the Wreys being now
people of some note—Marion had half-a-dozen
invitations for this particular evening, she
preferred spending it at home and alone.
She sat thinking of many things, past and
present, but most of all of Cuthbert's changed
manner of late. It had for some time been
a source of great uneasiness to her. He did
not complain or show any sign of illness;
he was sanguine as to the outcome of public
affairs; his ambition was not so high as to
ensure disappointment. What, then, had
changed him—changed his way of speaking,
changed his smile? Could it be, she thought,
with the quick suspicion of a loving woman,
that his affection for her was waning? Did
he at last begin to think that, in marrying
one so lowly as herself, he had thrown a
chance away? But such thoughts were but
passing ones. He had given her too many

proofs of the endurance of his love to permit
her to harbour such unworthy doubts. Yet
she sighed, and prayed that whatever
weighed upon her husband's mind might be
removed, or that he would let her share the
burden. After a while she rose and rang
the bell.

'Bring me to-night's letters,' she said.

Cuthbert kept no secretary. He was an
energetic man, equal to any amount of work ;
but whilst the House was sitting, his correspondence was so voluminous that, recently,
his wife opened many of his letters and
sorted them according to the importance
they bore. In this way she saved him much
time.

There was a goodly pile to-night. She
opened and examined each letter in turn—
all save one or two which she laid aside un-
touched, knowing, from the initials on the
envelopes, that they contained political matter
so weighty, that she must not be the first to
read it. Presently she came upon a thick
packet, sealed and registered. It bore the
Liverpool post-mark, and was marked
'Private'—but so was every second enve-

lope.   Without hesitation she broke the
cover and drew the letter out, leaving the
other papers which accompanied it behind.

'A begging petition with testimonials,' she
said as she opened the letter, preparing
to take a hasty glance at its contents.   As
she unfolded the paper, a small bright object
dropped from it on to her lap.   It was a gold
cross, one arm of which was broken off.   She
took it in her hand, looked at it for a moment,
and then started as if a snake had bitten her.
With the trinket still in her hand, she turned
to the letter, and her face grew paler with
every line she read.

The missive was short; its meaning must
have been plain, as Marion had no need to
reperuse it.   As she read the last word, she
let both letter and trinket fall, then, uttering
a low cry of pain, placed her hands upon her
eyes.

'O my darling!' she moaned, 'and is this
the reason ?—this is why you have changed
so, lately ! My love, I may have deserved it,
but not like this !'

So she sorrowed for a time ; then her mood

changed. She rose, and dashing her tears away, paced the room like a queen.

'If an angel had told me this, I would have laughed him to scorn! After so many years —so many happy years! Cuthbert, Cuthbert! why did you do it? How could you do it? It was your right to know. Had you wished it, I would have told you—told you freely, in spite of your promise. But oh! to learn it like this, through a hired spy!'

Then her proud bearing forsook her, and the hot tears sprang forth again. But at last she grew composed; but there was a world of sweet regret in the words she addressed to her absent husband:

'Yes, you will still love me, and I shall forgive even this. But never, never again shall we be the same to each other—never quite the same, Cuthbert!'

She looked at the contents of the packet. Two or three letters in a woman's handwriting—one well known to her—which gave her the feeling as of ghosts rising from the past. She replaced everything in the cover, and locking it away, sat late into the night,

thinking and thinking — longing for the
morrow to end her suspense.

The next day, Cuthbert returned just in
time to greet her for a moment before he
went down to the House. He had a question on the notice paper, one that, he knew,
would stick like a barbed arrow into the
Home Secretary's well-seasoned flank. He
was in better spirits than usual.

'We shall smite them hip and thigh!' he
cried. 'Inside their own fortresses we shall
slay them!—My darling, how ill you look.
What is the matter?'

'I have passed a bad night,' she faltered.
She could not reproach him at that moment.
She could not understand why, with that
letter waiting for him, his voice should
express such unmistakable anxiety and soli-
citude.

'Lie down, dearest,' he said, 'and rest till
I come home. I shall be back to dinner.'

He kissed her, and went to St. Stephen's.
Except for the fear as to what news any
post might bring him from his detective, he
was very joyous. Every paper had a leader
on the speeches of last night, and his speech

had been an important and favourably criti-
cized one.

He was in good spirits when he came home
to dinner. His bout with the Home Secretary had succeeded to a marvel. His manner
to Marion, who still looked worn and weary,
had never been more affectionate. She felt
bewildered.

Dinner over, he must go to his duties
again. She could not let the moment pass.
She placed herself in a low chair near him—
her favourite seat.

'Must you go to the House to-night,
Cuthbert ?'

' I don't know about " must." I ought to,
although there will be no division of importance. If you feel ill, my darling, I will stay
with you.' He kissed her so lovingly, that
she knew it could be no pretence, and wondered more and more. ' How cold your lips
are,' he said. ' Yes ; I will stay with you to-
night.'

She thanked him, but waited a while, as in
deep thought, before she spoke again.

'Cuthbert,' she said, sweetly but gravely,
' may I tell you a little tale of real life ?'

He looked at her, and felt sure there was some grave meaning in her request.

'By all means,' he said.

Calm as she forced herself to be, her heart beat and her hand trembled as she drew out the little broken gold cross and placed it in his hand. He looked at it and then at her inquiringly.

'That was given me, years ago,' she said with an effort, 'by the man who was my husband, or who I fancied was my husband.'

Cuthbert started.

'Wait a moment, Marion. I did not ask for this. I do not want it. But if you wish to tell me, tell me with your hand in mine; for I swear that whatever you may choose to let me know shall make no difference between us.'

His voice was passionate as when he first pleaded for her love.

She did not understand. She looked at him almost dreamily, but did not place her hand in his.

'No, Cuthbert. It may be I shall have a question to ask you. Let me tell it my own way.'

He saw she was quite serious, so listened
with growing fear.

'I was but a girl,' she said, very quietly
and with her eyes cast down—'a girl of
twenty.   He told me he loved me.   He was
young, and, I believed, would change his
manner of life for my sake.   I married him.
For a few months I was happy; then I
found him as he really was—a false liar, a
coward, a swindler.   When years afterwards
he told me I was not even his wife—that
even in that he had deceived me—I think, in
spite of the shame, my heart leapt for joy.
He could claim me no more.—Did I wrong
you, my Cuthbert, by marrying you?   I was
only sinned against.   My silence must have
made you think it even worse than this.—
Now, I will give you your letter.'

Cuthbert was very grave.

'Why do you tell me this, Marion?   I
was of course bound to guess at something
of the kind.   Why tell me now?   I never
asked; I never wished to know.'

He had not noticed her mention of the
letter, nor would he have known what she
meant by it.   She drew it from her breast.

'My husband,' she said sadly, as she handed it to him, 'we can never be quite as we were before you did this thing. If you doubted, why not have asked me? Why not have asked Mr. Mayne? I will not reproach you, but you have degraded both me and yourself.'

He took the letter in stupid astonishment. That he and Marion were at cross-purposes, that she was under some delusion, was evident. What it was he could only learn from reading the letter, so, without another word, he read:

'DEAR SIR,

'I would have seen you, but am ordered away on an affair of great import-ance. I do not neglect your interests in going. A child might now follow the clue. Winslow and his wife lived for some time at D——. He left her—deserted her, prob-ably, when he sailed for the States. She lived on at D—— for a while, trying to make an income by keeping a small school. Then she fell seriously ill, and at last was taken away by a gentleman, whose

15—2

name my informant forgets, but who was Rector of St. Winifred's, a church on the outskirts of London. This should be ample for your purpose ; but I enclose some letters and a trinket left behind her when she quitted the house at which she lodged.'

As he finished the letter and read the signature of his confidential agent, Cuthbert's head felt in a whirl. It was some little time before he could see the connection between his wife's grief and this letter which brought the dreaded moment close to hand. His first thought was that Marion was troubled by his having concealed the matter from her.

He glanced at the letter once more, and this time the mention of St. Winifred's arrested his attention. The whole truth came to him like a flash of lightning. Astonishment no longer expressed his state. He stared at his wife. She stood with her eyes cast down, her beautiful face pale and sad, and with tears slowly running down her cheeks.

'But the child !' gasped Cuthbert—'your child !'

Still ignorant of the truth, she looked at
him with reproachful eyes. Why should he
wish to probe every old wound ?

' Poor little baby !' she said ; ' poor little
boy ! The only thing in all that time I can
look back to with a happy thought—the only
gleam of sunshine in my life. But he died,
Cuthbert—died before I wrote to my old
friend Mrs. Mayne, begging her to come
and save me from starvation or worse.
Then it was I said, " I will have no past." '

Cuthbert rose and clasped his wife to his
heart. Had she wished to resist, those
strong loving arms of his would have made
resistance useless.

' Marion, my wife, my darling !' he cried,
' can you not understand ? I have been
sending across the world to find traces of
the widow and son of Ralph Blatchford, to
whom, if I could have done what was right,
I must have given up nearly every farthing
of the wealth we enjoy ; and from this letter
I learn that Ralph Blatchford was the man
who married you under the assumed name
of Winslow ! Marion, if you understood
what this means to me, to you, to the

children, you would be happier than ever
you have been before !'

Marion understood.

She laughed a half-delirious but entirely
happy laugh ; her hand stole into her husband's, and the whole question of the
Blatchford bequest was ended, and at rest
for ever.

MY FIRST CLIENT.

(A SOLICITOR'S TALE.)

CHAPTER I.

'MR. BROWNLOW, sir,' said my small clerk, opening my office door.

'Show him in,' I said, covering with a bulky draft the novel which I was reading.

Then my first client stood before me.

My first client! In spite of the bundles of documents, docketed, endorsed, and arranged in due order; in spite of the litter of papers in front of me; in spite of other clever devices which I hoped gave my office the look and odour of good substantial legal business, until now I was clientless.

It is true I had not long been practising on my own account. Ten days, if I remem-

ber rightly; but those ten days, during which
I waited for business to come to me, were
the dullest and dreariest in my life. I was
beginning to despair. I did not even know
from which quarter to expect business. Far
away in the dim future I saw a possibility of
being employed to draw up a marriage settle-
ment. The landlord of the house in which
I lodged was in hot dispute with his neighbours about the right of using a pump, and
had sounded me as to the probable cost of
legal proceedings. With these exceptions, I
had nothing to look forward to when my first
client made his appearance.

An elderly, delicate-looking man ; his eyes
blue, with a kind, mild expression in them ;
his hair light and thin. Evidently a timid,
halting, irresolute man, of no strength of
character. Born, not to command, but to be
bullied by wife, son, daughter, or anybody
with whom he came in contact. Stooping
somewhat, as if accustomed to yield to
storms, not to resist them. Speaking hesi-
tatingly and respectfully, with a plaintive
inflexion in his voice. Clothes good, but
old-fashioned.

Such was my first client.

I begged him to be seated, then waited to hear why he came.

'I want a little matter attended to,' he said. 'Mr. Johnson, of High Street, advised me to come to you.'

Johnson was my bootmaker—I registered a vow of gratitude, to be discharged by future orders; then, bowing in acknowledgment, asked my client what he required.

It was, as he said, a small matter. An agreement for a lease of a house which he was about letting. His name I found was James Brownlow; his address, Vine Cottage, North Road; his description, retired builder —in legal phraseology, gentleman.

So far as the grave and learned air which I was bound to assume permitted, I made myself very pleasant and affable to him. He listened to my words with deference, agreed to all my suggestions, wished me a respectful good-morning, and went his way.

Of course I told him my hands were so full of business that it was impossible for me to get the agreement prepared under two days. At the time appointed he called with his tenant, paid me my modest costs, and disappeared for the space of several months.

When next I saw him, he brought me something well worth having. He had sold some houses, and wished to invest the proceeds by way of mortgage, so that my second bill of costs was of a respectable length and of a comforting amount. From what he told me I found that he possessed, one way and another, a good deal of property. How he could have made his money was to me a mystery. Judging from his timid and yielding disposition, I should have thought him the last man in the world to get on. I suppose our fathers made money much more easily than their sons do, in these days of cut-throat competition and mortgage-broking—But let that pass. I, for one, must not complain—now.

One evening I passed Vine Cottage. My client was at the gate, and begged me to enter. His house was a pretty one, built by himself, and surrounded by a large well-kept garden. I found that whatever energy he did possess was devoted to horticulture. Plants being gentle, unresisting organizations, no doubt he was able to cope with them successfully. He was proud of his flowers, but even more so of his grapes, one variety of which, he told me, had become famous under the name of ' Brownlow's Seedling.'

As I am fond of gardening, and know something about it, the old man seemed to find a kindred spirit in mine, so much so that, after our inspection of the garden and the greenhouses, he urged me to stay to supper with him. I had another engagement, but, as my new friend seemed likely to be such a good client, I felt I ought not to neglect the opportunity, so I accepted the offer, and entered the house.

At the supper-table I found two middle-aged women, his daughters. The elder, I learned, was a widow; the younger, unmarried. I already knew that my client's wife had been dead many years, and from the conversation at the table I gathered that the widowed daughter had two or three children. Afterward, I ascertained that she and her family lived with Mr. Brownlow, who supported them all.

As I inspected my new acquaintances, I

decided that in appearance and disposition they must take after their deceased mother, and argued that, if my supposition was correct, the late Mrs. Brownlow was not the pleasantest of her sex. Father and daughters were never less alike. The latter were two tall, bony, hard-faced women, and as I noticed that when Mr. Brownlow spoke to them his manner was more timid, his speech more hesitating than ever, I felt sure I had not missed my mark when I summed him up as a man much bullied by his nearest relatives. It was easy to see that the poor old fellow's womankind ruled him with a rod of iron—a domestic sceptre no doubt handed down together with traditions of home tyranny from mother to daughters. He seemed to smoke his pipe surreptitiously; to drink his whisky and water apologetically; to laugh guardedly; in fact, in his daughters' presence, to do all things with the hope of approval, or the fear of correction before his amiable eyes.

To me, the ladies, although patronizing, as became our respective positions, were civil enough. When I said good-night, they were good enough to hope to see me again at Vine Cottage. 'When we trust,' added the widow, 'to entertain you better—but having expected no one,' etc. In spite of fair words, I did not like them. They were too severely moulded to suit me, and I felt sure that the moment my back was turned poor old Brownlow would be taken to task for having invited a guest without notice to his joint sovereigns.

After this visit to Vine Cottage I saw my old client frequently, both at my office and out of doors. If I passed his house of an evening I generally found him at the gate, anxious that I should enter and admire some new floral triumph. Through the kindness of a friend I had been able to present him with some choice varieties of several of his pet plants. He was absurdly grateful. Perhaps even a trifling act of spontaneous kindness was a new experience to him. Sometimes, not often, I spent the evening with him, and each time I did so, and saw him in the company of his sour-looking daughters, I was more confirmed in my opinion that he was very unkindly treated at home. At last I grew to dislike the oppressors as much as I pitied and liked the oppressed, whom I found so gentle, kind, and hospitable, that, leaving all mercenary considerations out of the question, I began to entertain a sincere regard for him.

One morning, to my surprise, his widowed daughter, Mrs. Wrench, paid me a visit. If either of my client's daughters was sourer, harder-looking—in fact, more objectionable than the other—it was Mrs. Wrench. She was a hungry-looking woman, with long teeth and high cheek-bones. She was always dressed in black, but her garments looked old and rusty. Out of doors she wore black thread gloves, the touch of which set my teeth on edge. She entered my office, and after giving me her rasping, rigid hand, seated herself.

' My father would have called himself, Mr. Carr,' she began, ' but did not feel equal to the walk.'

' I hope he is not ill,' I said politely.

' No, not exactly ill; but upset by an unpleasant family matter.'

' Can I be of any service to him ?'

'Yes. He wishes you to write a letter—
at once; so he asked me to call and give you
instructions.'

I bowed, and waited the instructions.

' You will ₁please write to-day,' she said,
in her incisive, metallic voice, her ill-favoured
face growing harder as she spoke. ' You
will write to Mrs. Richard Brownlow, 18,
Silver Street, and say that no further appli-
cation she makes to Mr. Brownlow will be
noticed. Say also,' she added, ' that Mr.
Brownlow, in justice to others, is seriously
thinking of reducing the amount he has for
some years been in the habit of sending her.'

Whoever Mrs. Richard Brownlow might
be—whether her claim on my client were just
or unjust—such a peremptory refusal, written
by a solicitor, admitting of no appeal and
ending with a threat, was so much at variance
with my old friend's easy and vacillating
nature, that I hesitated.

' I am clearly to understand, Mrs. Wrench,
that these are Mr. Brownlow's expressed
wishes ?'

She snapped her thin lips, and looked at
me in a manner far from pleasant.

'Undoubtedly, Mr. Carr — moreover, he
wishes you to write at once. Let there be
no delay, if you please.'

'If you please' is an innocent-looking
phrase, but the expression Mrs. Wrench
threw into those words was most significant.
Considering it had settled the matter, the
hard-faced widow rose, gathered up her rusty
skirts, and bade me a severe good-day.

'Now, who may Mrs. Richard Brownlow
be?' I said, as her angular, ungracious form
vanished through the green baize door.
'Some poor relation asking for help, I suppose. I doubt very much whether the old
man knows anything about the appeal, and I
dare say my instructions emanate only from
the charming Mrs. Wrench.'

Nevertheless, I wrote the letter; my not
doing so would, I felt sure, make a bitter
enemy of Mrs. Wrench, and enemies were
luxuries which I could not yet afford. If I did
wrong in following her instructions, I could
throw all the blame on her shoulders. So
the next post took my letter to the address
she gave me—a poo street in a poor part of
the town.

Chapter II.

AT the end of the week Mr. Brownlow called, looking more timid and nervous than ever. He said nothing about the letter, but having finished discussing the business which I was conducting for him, fidgeted about and seemed very ill at ease. He made contradictory remarks about the harvest and the crops, and could not, apparently, make up his mind whether to go or to stay. Presently he reseated himself, and dropping his voice to a whisper, said :

'Will you do me a kindness, Mr. Carr ?'

I begged him to command me in any way.

'I feel it is not quite the right thing to ask,' he said, with a feeble attempt at a laugh, 'but will you allow your clerk to take a cab and go with a letter for me ? He will bring some one back. It will only be a little girl. Perhaps you would not mind my seeing her here for a few minutes ?'

'He shall go at once,' I said ; 'but where is the letter ?'

'I must write it.'

Therewith, after spoiling several sheets of
my paper, he completed to his satisfaction a
short note.   It was addressed Mrs. Richard
Brownlow, 18, Silver Street.

'You know I wrote to this lady a few days
ago, by your request ?' I asked.

'Yes, yes—I know it,' he replied sadly.
'My daughters insisted.   No doubt they are
right, for they are good daughters, Mr. Carr,
and have never yet given me a moment's
trouble.   Oh yes, my daughters are always
right; but I want to see the little girl.'

I gave my clerk the letter and instructions.
When I returned, Mr. Brownlow was saying
to himself :

'Yes, I must see the little girl.   Richard's
little girl.'

'Your expected visitor is a relation of
yours ?' I asked.

'My granddaughter.   My poor son Dick's
child.   Dick went wrong, Mr. Carr.   I can't
think why he should have gone wrong,' he
added plaintively ; 'he never had a harsh or
unkind word from me.'

This I quite believed; but I wondered
if a few harsh words at the proper season

might not have prevented his son from going wrong.

'Yes, he disgraced us all,' continued the old man. 'Then he married and made matters worse. His wife was not the wife for such as Dick. Then he quarrelled with me, and said such things that I was obliged to alter my will and leave him nothing—but that was only to try and break his spirit, Mr. Carr. Then he left me in anger and went abroad. I never saw him again. He took to drinking, they told me, and soon died. He was a terrible disgrace and trouble, but he was my only son, and I should like to see the little girl.'

'Have you never seen her?'

'Never. Dick's widow has only just returned to the town. Since Dick's death I have been allowing her something, although my daughters say she has no claim on me; but I could not let her starve. Now she has written for more money, to give the child a proper education, she says. But I cannot be expected to do that, can I, Mr. Carr?'

He spoke timidly, as though my decision was a matter of great moment.

I knew it was not what he could do, but what my friend Mrs. Wrench and her sister would allow him to do.

' Better wait and see what your grandchild is like,' I suggested.

'Yes, yes, so I will,' he said, brightening up. ' But, Mr. Carr, you will say nothing about this at home ?'

I reassured him, whilst marvelling at his weakness. Soon the door opened, and my clerk led in a girl of about twelve years of age.

A pretty, winning child, with bright eyes, long soft hair, and an intelligent face. Her dress, although of poor material, neat and well fitting. I was able to trace in her young features a certain likeness to my client. Perhaps her natural timidity and shyness at entering a strange room and finding strangers awaiting her made the resemblance more apparent.

Mr. Brownlow held out his hand. The little maid went up to him, and after dropping an old-fashioned courtesy, put her small fingers into his.

'And what is your name, my dear ?' he asked kindly.

' I am Miss Lilian Brownlow, sir.'

' Lilian—Lilian,' repeated the old man.
' A very pretty name, too ; and do you know
who I am ?'

' You are my poor papa's papa,' she
replied. ' Mamma said I should see you if I
went with the young gentleman.'

' What else did your mamma tell you ?'
asked Mr. Brownlow, rather unfairly.

' She said I was to be very good, and then,
perhaps you would give her the money to
send me to a beautiful school.'

Old Brownlow looked very foolish as he
heard this candid avowal. He twisted in his
chair, and his eyes appealed to me for assistance.

' She is very like you,' I said, to create a
diversion.

He seemed pleased at my remark, and
placing his hands on her shoulders, looked at
her attentively and kindly.

' Like me, is she ? Well, she is like Dick.
She has his eyes, and people always said
Dick was like his father.'

' Suppose I can't send you to school,' he
asked the child, ' will you give me a kiss all
the same, my pretty one ?'

'Yes, I will give you a kiss,' she said, looking half inclined to cry.

She held up her little red mouth : the old
man kissed it many times, then placed her on
his knee and put his arms round her.   They
made quite an affecting group.   In the child's
interests, and feeling sure that I should put
a spoke in Mrs. Wrench's wheel, I thought it
better to leave them, so I quitted my office
for awhile.

In an hour's time I returned and found
them the best of friends.   With many kisses
Mr. Brownlow once more gave Lilian in
charge of the young gentleman, my clerk.
He saw them safely off, then returned to me.
For once he spoke like a man whose mind
is made up.   It was clear that his pretty
granddaughter had found a short cut to his
heart.   Memories of his dead son, loving and
pleasant ones, had arisen and erased his faults.
The child bore his name, and, Mrs. Wrench
notwithstanding, he felt that something must
be done for her.

'Mr. Carr,' he said, 'kindly write to Mrs.
Brownlow and tell her to send the child to
Miss H—'s school.   The bills can be sent to

you, if you don't mind the trouble of settling them. Also tell Mrs. Brownlow that you are instructed to pay her ten pounds every quarter in addition to what she now receives from me. Perhaps,' he added, with a return of his old manner, ' it would be well to make some inquiries as to what kind of woman she is—my daughters say such strange things about her.'

I promised to carry out his wishes, and expressed my pleasure that the child had found such favour in his eyes.

' A sweet little thing !' he said. ' A good, clever little child ! I only wish I could take her home to live with me—but there are obstacles—and very likely she would not be happy,' he added, as if thinking aloud.

I did not put my thoughts into words, but I agreed with him. There were obstacles, and, even if Mr. Brownlow could attack and surmount them, they must impede the march of the little interloper's happiness.

Although he dared not take the child home —although he never went near Silver Street —Mr. Brownlow continued to see Lilian frequently. He made my office quite a con-

veniency.   He usually called there on Wed-
nesday and Saturday afternoons, the girl's
half-holidays, and, with many apologies for
the liberty he was taking, despatched my
clerk in search of her.   Then they sallied
forth together.   It was his custom to take a
cab, drive some distance into the country,
alight, and ramble about the fields until it
was time to return home.   I laughed as I
drew mental pictures of the state in which
the amiable Mrs. Wrench and her sister would
be if they should chance to learn how their
father employed so much of his time.   As
yet they had discovered nothing, although
years had gone by, and the girl was growing
tall, and bidding fair to become an attractive
and accomplished young lady.

My client had several times spoken to me
about making a fresh will and providing for
Lilian, but as yet nothing had been done.
Although I had tried to do so, I had not
been able to get any definite instructions from
him.   I believe he was deterred by that
absurd superstition which influences more
men than one would think, that a will should
not lightly be meddled with—making a new

one or altering an old one being often the precursor of a quick decease. It was to be made—it should be made—yet it was not made. The friendly relations now existing between us allowed me to hint to him that in case of his death Lilian and her mother would be penniless. He quite saw the force of my remarks, yet he still hesitated and postponed. How many men have done the same thing, and the ones whom they loved best in life have suffered from the foolish delay !

CHAPTER III.

SOME two years after Lilian made her first appearance, three half-holidays in succession passed without my client paying me his usual visit. My clerk—the original young gentle-man, for I had more than one clerk now—looked out for him wistfully. Probably certain half-crowns which from time to time changed hands were a welcome addition to his weekly stipend, or it may be that, in his secret heart, the youth nourished tender feelings towards his little charge. Such a protracted absence being unprecedented, I called at Vine Cottage to learn what was the cause of it. One of the daughters received me, and informed me her father was ill. He had been in bed several days. Was he seriously ill ? They feared so. Was he conscious ? Yes, but very weak. Could I see him ? Utterly out of the question—he was too ill to see anyone.

The woman's manner made me dread the worst. I thought of that graceful child, who had grown so dear to the old man, thrust back into poverty. Her mother and herself, at the best, kept from sheer starvation by what small pittance might be wrung from the stony sisters. I pitied the mother almost as much as the child, for the result of the inquiries which I had instituted by Mr. Brownlow's request showed her to be of undoubted respectability. A factory girl originally, whose pretty face had caught Richard Brownlow's fancy ; but a girl, evidently, with thoughts and ideas above her class. Poor woman, she had suffered much ! Her husband had ill-used her, and during Lilian's early years her life had been one hard struggle. The two last years must have been the happiest since her marriage; they were at least free from anxiety and semi-starvation. And now, if old James Brownlow died, all her misery must begin again.

So I begged as his friend and legal adviser to be allowed to see him, if only for a moment. Whilst I urged my request, the second daughter entered the room and joined her sister in an absolute refusal. So rigid and unbending was their attitude, that I feared they must suspect something of the truth. I tried them every way I could think of, but without getting them to yield an inch. The doctor, they said, had utterly forbidden it.

'Will you allow me,' I said, 'to wait until the doctor comes? I can show him how necessary it is that I should see Mr. Brownlow.'

'Certainly not,' replied Mrs. Wrench, with a face of adamant. 'Not with my consent shall my poor father's last hours, it may be, be disturbed by matters of business.'

'Certainly not,' echoed her sister.

Entreaty failing, I turned to craft. Taking
my hat, I rose, shrugging my shoulders like
one who had cleared his conscience by trying
to do his duty.

'As you like, my dear ladies ; but I must
not be blamed by-and-by. I can only say
that, unless I speak to him to-day, it may
make a great pecuniary difference to your-
selves.'

This was true enough, but not exactly as
I meant them to understand it.

The shaft went home.   I had touched the
key-note — avarice.   They glanced at each
other, and held a whispered consultation.   I
hoped I had outwitted them ; but two such
women are more than a match for the sharpest
lawyer on the rolls.

' Mr. Carr,' said the widow, ' if you choose
to tell us the exact facts of the case, we will
decide if they justify our running the risk.'

She snapped up her thin lips and gave me
a searching glance.

' No, I cannot do that.   The business is of
a private nature.   Many interests are in-
volved.   You must take my word for its
vital importance.'

The sisters exchanged a look which plainly said, ' I told you so.' Mrs. Wrench folded her huge bony hands on her sombre lap.

' Then, sir,' she said, ' you will not see him. What secrets can a father wish to keep from his daughters ?'

' We don't believe a word of your tale,' added the other most offensively.

' If there is any secret,' continued Mrs. Wrench venomously, ' perhaps this letter, found by us a few days ago, has something to do with it.'

She handed me a letter. It was in a girlish handwriting, and ran thus :

' DARLING GRANDPA,—

    ' I have a bad cold and cannot come to-day.

            ' With love and kisses, your

                        ' LILIAN.'

Then they knew or guessed everything. Poor little Lilian !

' Answer me, sir !' cried Mrs. Wrench, stamping her heavy foot. ' Who is Lilian ? That shameful woman's child, I suppose ? Is it on her account you want to see my father ? Is she your important business ? Answer me !'

I was spared the task. The door opened suddenly, and in staggered a feeble, wasted figure, clothed in an old dressing-gown. It was my client. He sank into the nearest chair, and panted for breath.

I needed no doctor to tell me that my poor old friend's hours were numbered. He had, in the course of some ten days, wasted away almost to nothing. Death was written legibly on his white and ghastly face. He seemed so exhausted that the fear came over me that, then and there, his eyes would close for ever.

His daughters, spell-bound by the turn events had taken, gazed at each other in blank astonishment. Even in that moment I was able to exult in their discomfiture. I ran to the sideboard, where, luckily, stood a spirit-case and glasses. I poured out a glass of brandy. The dying man drank a little and revived.

'Go,' he said hoarsely, waving his thin hand towards his daughters. 'Go—at once.'

Frightened as the women were, they kept their seats in sullen defiance.

'Go,' he said again. 'Go ; or, by heaven !

Mr. Carr shall make a will and leave everything to the hospital.'

His voice was low, and he spoke with difficulty; but words and accent were so stern and fierce that I could scarcely believe I was listening to my timid, hesitating old friend.

His daughters, doubtless even more surprised than I was, left the room, muttering their dissatisfaction. My client sank back in his chair.

'Lock the door,' he whispered. I did so. Then he laid one wasted hand on mine.

'Thank God, you have come at last. I expected you every moment for days past.'

'I had no idea you were ill, Mr. Brownlow.'

'They told me they had sent and written. They said you were from home.'

'I have had no letter, and have not been out of town for weeks.'

'Then they lied. They let me see no one. Until three days ago I did not know I must die. Even that they kept from me. I heard your voice, and just managed to creep downstairs. I was bound to see you before it was too late.'

The moisture rose to his brow. He looked so faint that I made him swallow more brandy.

'Make a codicil,' he said. 'Leave my pretty girl all—leave her all.'

'Not all, surely! I said, surprised.

He relapsed into his familiar hesitation and uncertainty of purpose.

'No—no,' he said, 'not all. They have been good daughters. No ; leave my darling girl, my poor Dick's child, six thousand pounds.'

'I will draw up a codicil at once,' I said, looking round for pen and paper. His procrastinating habit still clung to him.

'No, not now,' he said. 'I am better. Perhaps I shall get well. But bring it to-morrow morning, that I may sign it and make sure.'

I had no intention of letting death forestall me, so, without heeding his words, I began to write. Before I had finished two lines I saw that my old client had fainted.

I tried, without success, to revive him. With a heavy heart I went for help. Mrs. Wrench was in the passage. Her ear, I felt sure, had that moment left the keyhole. Her sister stood just behind her. The looks they gave me showed what they thought of my proceedings.

We carried Mr. Brownlow to his bed. The servant ran for the doctor, and I left to prepare the codicil, praying the while that Mr. Brownlow might find strength of mind and body enough to insist upon seeing me in the morning.

At nine o'clock the next morning I was at Vine Cottage, and was not at all surprised when I was curtly refused admittance. I waited until the doctor paid his visit, accosted him before he entered, and begged him to aid me, or at least to let his patient know that I was outside. He would promise nothing, and his manner told me that the account he had received of last evening's events prejudiced me in his eyes. No doubt more lies were told him on this visit, for when he came out of the house he was good enough to inform me that he thought such unprofessional conduct as mine must damage any young solicitor. I kept my temper, and endeavoured to make him understand the facts of the case. He refused to listen to me.

'At least you will tell me how you find Mr. Brownlow this morning,' I said.

'As bad as can be. He has but a few hours to live.'

'Then,' I said, 'by refusing to aid me you doom the one he loved best in the world to utter poverty.'

'I have nothing to do with family dis-putes,' he said coldly, as he closed the door of his brougham and drove away.

I left the house, but returned there several times during the day. Each time I was denied entrance. I was at my wits' end. Bribery and corruption of servants was out of the question, as the door was always opened by Mrs. Wrench or her sister. No legal process would enable me to enter; and a forcible invasion for such a purpose as mine would, I felt certain, ruin us if the matter came to litigation.

At last I grew sick and weary of the whole thing. I went home determined to try again to-morrow, although I knew it would be useless unless Mr. Brownlow rallied in some unexpected manner, and grew strong enough to insist upon my being sent to him.

CHAPTER IV.

I LIVED at some distance from Vine Cottage. There were other lodgers in the house : the rooms over mine being occupied by a man with whom I was on very friendly terms. I had finished my tea and settled down to read, when Robinson came to my door, and asked me to join some friends of his in a rubber. I was not in the mood for society. I felt melancholy and upset. The faces of a dying man and a bright, happy child haunted me. I declined my friend's invitation, preferring to spend the evening with my book and my pipe. I read for a long, long time, undisturbed by the laughter which, at intervals of the game, I heard overhead. But read as hard as I would, I could not get Mr. Brownlow out of my thoughts. Perhaps at that very moment he was dying, and calling for me to carry out his wishes. I shuddered as I pictured the two hard-hearted mercenary women keeping watch over his bed, waiting for him to die. I saw them heeding his cries no more than stone figures might. Then, through my smoke - wreaths, rose Lilian's glad young face. How changed, I thought, it will look in six months' time, when privation and sorrow tell upon it. I blamed my old client bitterly for his folly. I blamed myself for not having urged him again and again until he made proper provision for the girl. Altogether, I knew the business had been badly managed, and felt miserable at my share in it.

The clock struck half-past eleven. I closed my book, and debated whether to go to bed or fill another pipe. At that moment I heard a knock at the street door. 'One of Robinson's friends come late,' I said. 'They mean to make a night of it.' I heard my landlady answer the summons ; then my door opened, and to my amazement—even horror —in walked Mr. Brownlow.

I thought I must be dreaming—the thing seemed impossible. Mr. Brownlow, the man yesterday evening scarcely able to totter downstairs—whose dying look had haunted me ever since—here, in my room—dressed as when last I saw him about! He looked as ill and ghastly as when I saw him in his own dining-room, but his step was not so feeble. The unexpected sight deprived me of speech and motion; the only sensation I was capable of feeling was wonder—wonder as to how he managed to reach my house. A man so enfeebled that only yesterday he fainted after walking a few steps and speaking a few words. It was inexplicable, but it was not impossible, for here he was!

I recovered my senses, and placed a chair for him. He seated himself wearily.

'My dear sir!' I said; 'surely this is most imprudent!'

He turned his head and looked at me.

What was it in that look that froze my blood—that made my hair rustle—that sent wild thoughts rushing through my brain? To this day I dare not answer the question; but something nameless was there—something which changed astonishment into sheer terror—such terror that for a moment my impulse was to rush out of the room and hide myself.

'I must sign that codicil to-night,' he said.

Although his voice sounded strange, it recalled me to myself.

It should be no fault of mine if the opportunity was lost. I took the document from my pocket and spread it out before him.

'Wait one minute,' I said : 'I must fetch witnesses.'

'You must be quick,' he answered, and his eyes again met mine. I shunned them, but as I left the room I felt that I was trembling in every limb.

Outside the door I could laugh at my fears. Robinson's card party was a lucky incident. I would go up and ask two of the players to act as witnesses. First let me get that codicil signed and attested : after that I could learn how Mr. Brownlow managed to reach my house.

Robinson and his friends raised a shout of welcome when I entered the room. I knew nearly every man there, and among the party were two solicitors of my acquaintance.

'I am sorry to disturb you,' I said apologetically, 'but would two of you come down and witness a will. Perhaps Thomas and Hicks '—my legal friends—' will spare me a minute.'

Thomas and Hicks laid down their cards and followed me to the door. Then a sudden thought occurred to me. The circumstances of the case were so unparalleled : a man leaving what was said to be his death-bed late at night to make a serious alteration in his will. If he died to-morrow, or in the course of a few days, this codicil would most certainly be disputed. Here were nine men. Let them all witness it. Such testimony might defy anything. So I turned and said :

'On second thoughts, as litigation is sure to come out of this, may I ask all of you to come down ?'

'Can't be too careful,' said Hicks approvingly, as the whole party rose and trooped after me.

'It's old Brownlow!' I heard Thomas whisper as we entered the room.

'So it is,' replied Hicks. 'They told me the poor old boy was dying.'

I handed my client a pen. As I did so

our hands met.   His touch sent an icy-cold
shiver through me.   He signed his name
pretty firmly.   His signature was duly
attested by Thomas and Hicks, whilst the
other men looked over their shoulders with
great curiosity.

Mr. Brownlow bowed to them politely,
whilst I thanked them for their services and
apologized for the trouble I had given them.
After wishing us good-night they went back
to their game.   I locked up the codicil and
then turned to question my client.

But the words died on my lips as I met
his eyes, and once more saw in them the same
mysterious, indescribable look which had
before so strangely affected me.   Again I
trembled from head to foot.

' I must go back,' he said, rising like one
wearied by some great exertion.

' Let me fetch a cab,' I said, recovering as
before when I heard his voice.

He shook his head, walked to the door,
opened it, and passed through.   I followed
him.   On the threshold he turned, and for
the last time his eyes met mine.   I sank on
a chair powerless, and, save for the throbbing

of my heart, motionless. The clock struck twelve.

In a few seconds, by a great effort, I forced myself to rise and go in pursuit of him. One way only led to his house. I ran along the road as fast as I could, but saw no sign of him. Thinking I must have passed him, I retraced my steps. He was nowhere in sight. I turned once more and ran on and on until I reached Vine Cottage. I rang the bell. The door was soon opened—it was evident that the inmates no longer feared assault. A maid, with her apron before her eyes, stood at the door.

'Has Mr. Brownlow come in?' I asked.

The girl stared at me stupidly. I repeated my question, adding that he had just left my house.

She did not seem to understand me.

'Master died at half-past eleven,' she said, again applying her apron to her tearful eyes.

He died at half-past eleven! Then I must be mad or dreaming. I went home. Robinson's card party was still in full swing. I unlocked my secretaire. There, safe and sound, was the codicil signed just before twelve o'clock! What could I think?

＊　　　＊　　　＊　　　＊　　　＊

The outcry raised by my notice of the existence of the codicil beggars description. The amiable sisters forced their way to my presence, and assured me nothing would satisfy them until I stood in the dock charged with forgery, conspiracy, and a few other crimes—their last penny should be spent to bring this about. Fortunately, the executors were men of business, and their solicitors men of honour who would not allow clients to go to law when they must lose. I had nothing to conceal, and it was soon ascertained that James Brownlow had signed the codicil in the presence of ten disinterested witnesses, leaving my landlady, who opened the door to him, out of the question. Every man who witnessed that signature was a respectable citizen, whose word would carry weight with judge and jury. Let the others swear that it was physically impossible for James Brownlow to leave his bed that night, we had overwhelming evidence that he did so—that he came to my house—that he signed the document. Moreover, our evidence was unbiased : theirs was tainted by animus and self-interest. I laughed as I thought whose shoulders eventually must bear the charge of conspiracy.

The law courts were never troubled with the matter. It was too simple. So, after some attempts at a compromise, which were sternly rejected, the legacy was paid, and the popular theory was that my client managed to slip from his bed unnoticed, and found strength enough to reach my house and ensure that his last wishes should be carried out.

It was years before I would exchange a word with the doctor who had lent so ready an ear to my calumniators. But he made me ample amends, and, at last, I forgave him. He told me a strange thing.

To all appearance his patient died at half-past eleven that night. The doctor went downstairs and talked to and comforted the women as best he could. Before leaving the house he went back to the chamber of death to look once more on the dead man. Whilst gazing on the peaceful face, the eyes sud-

denly opened, and the man he had pronounced dead gave a deep drawn sigh—a
sigh, it seemed, of relief—then the lids fell
again, and this time all was over.

'But,' said the doctor, 'I would swear in
any court of law that it was a simple impos-
sibility for him to have moved hand or foot.
Thank heaven I was not obliged to do so.
Your evidence was so overpowering that I
should have been ruined professionally. If
one believed in the supernatural, now——'

Just so. But, like the doctor, I don't
believe in it. Anyway, it is not as yet recognised by law. Nevertheless, the circumstances connected with my first client are
strange—very strange!

END OF VOL. I.

LONDON : REMINGTON AND CO.